VALENTINE VICTIM

KELLY HASHWAY

Contents

To Ayla with love

Chapter One

People just want to be heard and accepted—today more than any other day of the year. It's Valentine's Day. The holiday that makes single people feel lonely. In all honesty, it didn't take me becoming Dr. Sydney Warner, PHD. to figure that out. No, I learned that long before I became a psychologist. It's more like having my own private practice confirmed what I've always known. People like to be able to open up about their feelings and have someone genuinely listen. In a lot of ways, I often feel like a living, breathing diary. I exist for people to confide in without fear of others finding out. I'm a safe zone.

The problem is listening to everyone else's problems usually means I go home feeling like I'm carrying the weight of the world on my shoulders. It's hard not to feel their pain, experience their grief, and even assume their anger as my own. I close the door to my office and say goodnight to my receptionist, Lena Stillwater, who has been with me since I opened my private practice two years ago.

"Goodnight, Sydney. Have fun on your date."

I slam the heel of my hand to my forehead. "My date! I don't know how I forgot."

Lena cocks her head at me as she grabs her phone and car keys from the drawer. "Sydney, you've been talking about Malcolm Monaghan for weeks. How did you forget you were finally meeting him in person tonight?"

Probably because I still can't believe I signed up for a dating app in the first place. I blame my best friend, Autumn Young. She runs a youth center for troubled teens here in Swan Creek, but she can't let work go at the end of the day and decided to meddle in my personal life because she found my lack of dating to be troubling.

I resisted joining Kindred Hearts for months, but Autumn finally wore me down—mostly because I just wanted her to shut up about it. I didn't have high hopes the app would work, but then I met Malcolm.

He's a psychology professor, so we have something in common. He's also really easy to talk to. We mostly email because we're both busy with work, but we have talked on the phone a few times. He has a really deep voice that makes me smile every time he speaks. The tone is comforting, and I have no doubt he'd make a good motivational speaker.

Autumn is convinced Malcolm and I are perfect for each other, and after weeks of communicating, I'm finally ready to take the plunge and meet him in person.

"You better hurry up and get home so you have enough time to get ready," Lena says, pushing me out the door and toward my Nissan Altima.

"See you tomorrow," I tell Lena, getting into the car and immediately starting the engine. Luckily, I only live about nine miles from my office, so I'm home in fifteen minutes, which is when my phone rings.

I grab it off the bed where I tossed it as I assess my outfit options. Autumn's face fills the screen. "Hey, I'm struggling with what to wear," I answer.

"I figured as much. That's why I'm on my way over. I'll be there in ten minutes. That should give you plenty of time to shower."

"We have very different definitions of 'plenty of time,'" I tell her, heading for the bathroom. I end the call and turn on the water. After a long day of work, I like an almost equally long shower. Okay, that's an exaggeration, but I have been known to run out of hot water. No time for that tonight. I skip washing my hair because there's not enough time for that either. I'm just slipping my robe on when Autumn walks into my place.

"It's not fair that you're not married and you live in this incredible house, yet I am married and I live in an apartment."

"No luck with the house hunting?" I ask.

"Not yet. Aaron insists he needs a basement and an attic. Do you have any idea how difficult it is to find a home in this town with both?" She tosses her purse on the table in the entryway. "No chance you want to sell this place, huh?" She's always loved this house, but so have I.

"Sell the house my grandmother left me in her will? Not a chance. Sorry, hun. I love you, but it's not happening. Rumor has it a house in this development is going on the market, though. You might want to ask your realtor to get a jump on seeing it."

Autumn's eyes light up. "I will. Thanks."

"I'm pretty sure Mr. Jacoby has an attic. Not sure about the basement, though."

Autumn waves her hand in the air. "Enough about house hunting. Let me see your outfit options."

I lead her to the master bedroom where I have several options ranging from a classic black dress to jeans and a nice top.

"You're going to the park, right?" she asks.

"Yeah." We didn't want to go to a restaurant because it seemed way too cliché for Valentine's Day. And we didn't want the added pressure of everyone looking at us like we must be a couple in love when really we're meeting for the first time.

"So what made you pick a dress?" She grabs the hanger and walks the dress back to my closet.

"It's Valentine's Day. I mean, this might be our first date, but it's still a holiday."

"I get that, and I know you want to make a good first impression, but you also don't want to look uncomfortable and out of place. I'd go with the dark jeans and nice top. The turquoise in the shirt will bring out your eyes."

"Thanks." I grab both items and head back to the bathroom.

"Are you nervous?" she calls through the door.

"A little. I mean, Malcolm seems really great but how well can you get to know someone through email?" I slip into the jeans.

"You're the psychologist. You tell me."

I finish getting dressed and hang the robe on the back of the bathroom door before opening it. I plug in my flat iron to straighten the kinks in my hair from the clip I used to hold it up in the shower. Autumn makes a few adjustments to my makeup and then spins me to face the mirror.

"There," she says. "Perfect."

I don't know about perfect, but it looks like me staring back at me in the mirror, so it will do. "What time is it?"

"Time for you to leave. What do you have to bring?"

"Nothing. Malcolm said he had everything under control. I just have to show up at the park." I grab my phone to check the time. "How is it a quarter to eight already? I'm going to be late."

"Go. I'll lock up for you."

I start past her, but she grabs me and pulls me in for a hug. The look in her eyes when she releases me tells me exactly what she's thinking. "Don't go planning my wedding just yet, okay? You'll jinx it."

She holds both hands up in front of her. "I wouldn't dream of it."

I head for the front door.

"But you know," she says, following me. "It's not too late for us to have kids at the same time. I'm just saying. If things go well—"

"Good night, Autumn." I raise a hand over my head as I get into my car.

She stands in the doorway, watching me leave. She's like the sister I never had since I'm an only child. She is too, which is why we're so close. We lived next door to each other growing up, and unlike most of our classmates, we didn't move out of Swan Creek upon graduation. I stayed to finish my doctorate locally and to take care of my grandmother. Mostly to take care of my grandmother. And even now that she's gone, I can't leave. Living in her house makes me feel like she's still here. The psychologist in me did make me redecorate after Grandma Warner passed, though. The place now reflects my style instead of hers.

I connect to my phone's Bluetooth and click on my playlist. It's the one I use when I need to relax. I'm more nervous than I thought I'd be for this date, but then again, I haven't been excited to go on a date in a very long time. Taking care of Grandma Warner meant I had no time for a personal life. And before that, I was either working toward my doctorate or opening my own practice. There just hasn't been the opportunity to get serious about having a relationship until now. The thought scares me.

I pull into the parking lot and park under a street light. After cutting the engine, I take a few deep breaths and check my reflection in the rearview mirror. "You can do this, Sydney. It's only a date. And Malcolm is easy to talk to. Besides, it's a public place, so if he turns out to be a creep, I can walk away and be done with him." I nod to my reflection and open the car door.

The park gets a lot of traction at night. Many people come to walk the trail that surrounds the entire park. Others bring their dogs or their children to play. Seeing all the faces makes me relax. I probably know several people here, not that I want to run into any and have to endure an awkward conversation about being on my first date in years. No, thank you.

I put my head down and walk to the spot where Malcolm and I are supposed to meet. He chose the bench under the giant weeping willow tree. The bench is not fully out of view, but really only our feet and part of our legs will be visible to those passing by. So we'll have some privacy while still being partially in the open. I thought it was the perfect location.

On my way to the tree, a dog runs by me, his red leash trailing behind him. At the sound of the owner yelling, "Grab the leash!" I take off after the dog. It's not a big dog by any means. It appears to be some sort of basenji mixed breed.

"Here boy," I call to it.

It turns its head to look at me and stops running. Before it can get any ideas about taking off again, I bend down and grab the leash.

"Thank you!" a severely out of breath woman says as she catches up to us. "I've been chasing him for about fifteen minutes now."

I hand her the leash. "No problem. May I ask what breed he is?"

"Basenji and Jack Russell terrier. Basically, it adds up to quite the little devil."

I bend down to pet the dog on top of its head. "A very cute little devil, though, aren't you?"

"Careful, that's how he suckered me into adopting him," the woman says. "Thanks again."

"You're welcome." I stand up and do my best to pat my hair back into place after chasing the dog. Hopefully, I don't look too disheveled.

I'm nearly to the tree now, and each step seems harder and harder to take. I do a breathing exercise I have some of my patients do when they need to calm down, but my heart is still racing. No wonder they so frequently complain it doesn't work. Right now, I'm inclined to agree with them.

I take the last few steps to the outskirts of the tree. From here, I'll have to push some branches aside to get underneath the canopy of drooping branches.

"Now or never," I whisper to myself as I use my arms to separate some branches.

I should have expected it to be dark under here, but I thought Malcolm would have brought a lantern or some light source for us.

"Malcolm?" I call, walking toward where I know the bench will be. I grab my phone from my back pocket and turn on the flashlight. I keep it aimed at the ground so I don't accidentally trip over a tree root or step in dog poop—because let's face it; smelling like dog poop is not the best way to make a good first impression on a man I might like.

"Sorry, I'm late. I had to help a woman catch her dog whose leash got away from her." I raise the flashlight to the bench. "Malcolm?"

He's slumped awkwardly to the side, a discarded wine glass on the ground in front of the bench. Did he pass out drunk? I step toward him so I'm merely a foot away. "Malcolm," I say in a firm voice, annoyed that he'd drink himself unconscious on our first date.

When he doesn't respond, I lean closer. Something about his stillness, the way his chest isn't rising and falling sets me in a panic. I press two fingers to his neck to check for a pulse.

Nothing.

I inhale sharply and drop my phone. My date is dead.

Chapter Two

I don't know what to do. I've been to one funeral in my life. My grandmother's. And she was cremated, so this is the first dead body I've ever seen.

"Don't freak out, Sydney. Think." I try to look around, but I'm in complete darkness now. "My phone. Where did I drop it?" I bend down and reach all around on the grass until my fingers find the phone, which fell flashlight down. As soon as I raise it, Malcolm's lifeless form comes back into view. I shudder and move backward, not wanting to be too close to the body or alone with it for that matter.

As soon as I'm out from under the willow tree, I dial 911.

"911, what is the location of your emergency?"

"Swan Creek Park. I found a dead body under the giant willow tree."

"Did you say a *dead body*?"

"Yes. I checked for a pulse. There wasn't one."

"Ma'am, please remain on the line. I'm sending help right now."

"What should I do?" I ask, my voice shaking.

"Just stay where you are. Is anyone with you?"

"No, this was supposed to be a date. I was meeting him here." I swallow the lump in my throat.

"What is the victim's name?"

"Malcolm. Malcolm Monaghan. I just met him. Well, technically this was supposed to be our first meeting. We met on a dating app. We talked through emails mostly, and now… he's dead."

"Help should be to you any minute now. There's a police detective in the area."

I hear sirens in the distance. With every second they get louder, which means the police are getting closer. "I thought he was drunk," I tell the 911 operator. "He looked like he'd passed out, and there was wine."

"Ma'am, what's your name?"

"Dr. Sydney Warner. I'm a psychologist, and I admit I'm probably not handling this very well right now, but this is a first for me."

"I understand."

I give a nervous laugh. "You sound like me when I'm talking to patients."

The sirens stop, which mean the police must be here and parked. I look around, expecting to see people hurrying toward me. "I think they're here."

I spot Detective Lange coming toward me with a flashlight. He's a good ten years older than I am, but we've both lived in Swan Creek all our lives so we know each other by name. Not to mention his younger brother, Nolan, was only a year ahead of me in school. "Detective," I call to him. "Over here." I thank the 911 operator and end the call, returning the phone to my back pocket.

"Sydney Warner," Detective Lange says.

I nod. He was at my grandmother's funeral. Everyone in town loved my grandmother. She did make the best cookies, and she was known for bringing them to town meetings. She said nothing brought people together like good food. Preferably desserts. She wasn't wrong.

"He's on the bench. Under the tree." I point as if the massive tree isn't obvious to anyone with functioning eyes.

Detective Lange looks me up and down. "Stay there. Don't move."

I nod and watch him push the branches aside to walk under the tree. While I wait, some paramedics arrive. I don't have the heart to tell them they're too late. They can't help Malcolm now.

Detective Lange comes back out from under the tree. "Sydney, I'm going to need you to come down to the station with me."

I figured I'd have to answer a lot of questions since I'm the one who found Malcolm like this. "Of course. Now?"

He holds up one finger and then gets on his phone. He turns away from me so I can't hear his conversation, not that I'd try to eavesdrop anyway. I want this night to be over. What was supposed to be a promising date with a really nice guy has turned into a complete nightmare. I don't even know how Malcolm died. Was it a heart attack? Did people die of heart attacks at thirty-four? Or was Malcolm lying to me about his age when he said he was four years older than I am?

No, he doesn't look any older than thirty-four. I have to stop letting my mind race. That's not my job anyway. The police will determine cause of death.

Detective Lange turns back to me, his phone pocketed once again. "Did you drive here?"

"Yes, my car is in the parking lot. I can follow you back to the station." He's probably right. It's best to get this over with. Then I can put this awful night behind me. Moving on is healthy and exactly what I need to do.

Detective Lange looks like he's debating something.

"Drew?" I ask, hoping calling him by his first name will bring him out of whatever mental battle he has going on inside his head. "What is it?"

"Sydney, you should really come in my car. I can drive you back to yours later."

"Is that really necessary?" I ask. I'm doing him a favor. I found a dead body. My date's dead body. The weight of what's happening hits me. "Maybe you're right. I shouldn't be driving right now."

He takes me by my elbow and walks me through the park to his patrol car. He opens the door for me and gives me a sympathetic smile before walking around to the driver's seat. He doesn't say anything on the ride to the station. Neither do I. I'm not ready to talk about what happened yet. I need a moment to clear my mind. I take several deep, cleansing breaths in an attempt to calm myself, but they're as useless as blowing bubbles with my gum right now. A habit I never understood. It's a nervous tick, but usually the popping sound only worsens the situation for the chewer. Or at least that's the case for Thomas Moss, my standing Tuesday morning appointment. Not that he's taken my advice and ditched the gum. He'd rather pop it in my office as if trying to prove me wrong. The problem is it makes him more agitated. I should make a no gum chewing policy for the office. Lena could put up a sign for me.

"Sydney?" Detective Lange says, and I realize we're already at the station, and he's holding the car door open for me.

"Sorry. Thank you." I step out, and he closes the door behind me.

We walk into the station, and a few heads turn in our direction. Small towns mean lots of gossip. I'm sure everyone here already knows I discovered a body at the park. They all probably know I was supposed to be on a date with the man as well. I wonder if any of them are contemplating if it was suicide because Malcolm decided he couldn't bear the thought of dating me.

I shake my head. No. Now I'm acting like Thomas. I might as well ask Detective Lange if he has any gum for me. I need to keep my head on straight.

Detective Lange brings me to a room. "Have a seat."

I look around at the two-way mirror, single table with two chairs, and recording device in the middle of the table. "Wait. Is this an interrogation room?"

"Would you like some water?" Detective Lange asks.

"I'd like an answer. Why are we in an interrogation room?"

Detective Lange holds up a finger. "I'll be right back with some water. Just sit." He motions to the chair again in case I missed it the first time.

I have no idea what's going on. I thought we'd sit at his desk, and he'd ask me about how I found Malcolm. Or what time we were supposed to meet for our date. Questions you'd ask an innocent bystander who happened to have the unfortunate luck of having her Valentine's Day derailed because her date dropped dead.

How did Malcolm die? Was it the wine he was drinking? Was he allergic to something in it?

Detective Lange returns with a bottle of water and a file folder. He hands the water to me. "I see you still haven't sat down."

"I can't. I feel like I'm going to jump right out of my skin."

He motions to the water. "Drink. You'll feel better." He sits down and opens the folder.

"What's that?" I ask, trying to peer over his shoulder, but he closes the file again.

"Sydney, I must insist you sit now." He presses a button on the recording device on the table. "This is Detective Lange interviewing Dr. Sydney Warner in connection with the murder of Malcolm Monaghan."

"Murder?" I blurt out. "He was murdered? How? Why? Who would do this?"

"I'm hoping you can help me figure that out." He gestures to the seat, and this time I do sit because I'm tired of being told to like I'm a dog.

"How long have you known Malcolm Monaghan?"

"Um, about a month."

"Where did you meet?"

"Through the Kindred Hearts dating app." I wrap both hands around the water bottle.

"And when was the last time you saw him alive?"

"Never."

Detective Lange meets my gaze and cocks his head. "What do you mean never?"

"We'd never actually met before. We only talked online or on the phone. This was supposed to be our first date."

"A first date on Valentine's Day, the most romantic day of the year?" His tone couldn't be more skeptical.

"Well, it depends on how you look at the holiday. I have a lot of patients who would disagree with your definition of this particular holiday."

"I'm sure they would. Go on."

"Malcolm and I made plans to meet at the park at eight. He was taking care of the food and wine. I only had to show up, but when I did..." I pause and regroup. "I thought he was drunk at first. You know, like he was trying to get some liquid courage and overdid it. But then I realized his chest wasn't moving, so I checked to see if he had a pulse."

"You touched the body?"

"Yes, because I was afraid he wasn't breathing."

"And then what?"

"I called 911."

He nods and opens the file again. "How would you describe your relationship with the deceased?"

"We didn't really have a relationship, like I said. We'd just met. I don't even know much about him."

"I don't know if I'd say that's true. With social media these days, you can get to know someone pretty well without ever meeting in person."

Now it's my turn to cock my head. "Come on, Detective. We both know social media is designed for people to hide their true selves. Anyone can claim to be anyone or anything online."

"Is that why you agreed to meet him tonight? Were you unsure if he was being honest with you?"

"Actually, it was the opposite. I was pretty sure everything he'd told me about himself was true. I guess I felt like I could trust him, so why not meet him in person?"

"I'm assuming you two bonded over the fact that you both love psychology." His expression morphs into one you'd expect to see on a parent who catches their child with her hand in the cookie jar.

"It's something we have in common. Yes." I sit forward in my chair. "Where are you going with this?"

"Your job must admittedly be more taxing than his, though, right? I mean you listen to people's problems all day long. That has to be tiring. Whereas Malcolm taught psychology. When he went home for the day, he could leave his work… well, at work."

I lean back in the chair now. "Are you one of those people who thinks teachers have easy professions, because I have to say you're wrong there. I have a client who is a teacher. She always brings her work home with her. She cares deeply about her students."

Detective Lange clears his throat. "So you have a high opinion of teachers?"

"Yes. Of course."

"And you'd like to become one, wouldn't you?"

How would he know that? I've only told a select few that I'd like to teach one day. When I don't respond, he continues.

"The problem is you love this town and have no intention of moving. But getting jobs here can be difficult. Malcolm is too young to retire. You wouldn't get his position unless he decided to leave or something happened to him."

My mouth opens, but I can't find the words to express how I feel about what he just said. He's accusing me of murder. How did we go from me helping the police to me being accused of killing Malcolm? "You think I killed him to take his job? That's the most absurd thing I've ever heard. I'm already employed. It's not even like I need a job."

Detective Lange pulls a sheet of paper from the file in front of him and slides it across the table to me. "Do you deny writing this message to the deceased?"

I scan the contents of the paper. It's a printout of one of my emails with Malcom where I say I wish I could teach instead of listening to people's problems all day long. I remember I was in a particularly whiny mood that day after a client wouldn't leave my office. She just went on and on about how unfair life was and how no one had it as difficult as she did. I encounter a lot of people with that attitude in my line of work. I'm not sure why so many believe they're above the problems we all have to face on a daily basis. "Where did you get this?"

"One of my colleagues retrieved it from the victim's computer. Now answer the question. Do you deny writing that?"

What did they do, hack Malcolm's computer while Detective Lange drove me here? How did they get this so quickly? "No. I wrote it, but you don't understand."

Detective Lange holds up a hand. "I think I do. I think you saw this as an opportunity to get what you've always wanted."

"You think I joined a dating app to find a psychology professor I could kill so I could take his job? Are you even listening to yourself right now? I mean, what kind of police work is this? Where is there any proof? I'm the one who found Malcolm's body. If I killed him, why would I call it in to the police?"

"To avoid looking guilty." He leans forward, resting is forearms on the table between us and lacing his fingers together. "Maybe you thought you'd avoid suspicion if you were the one to call 911. It's smart thinking, actually."

I relax my shoulders because I'm not going to give him any body language he can interpret as the actions of a guilty woman. "Detective Lange, I don't know how you read Malcolm's email this quickly, or what would have even possessed you to, but I think you're trying to wrap this up so you can get home to your wife and salvage what's left of Valentine's Day."

His mouth hangs open for a split second, just long enough for me to know I hit home with that one.

"Look, I've told you everything I know. You clearly have my communications with Malcolm, so you don't need me for that either. Since you have no evidence that I did anything to harm Malcolm, and I don't even know how he was killed, you can't hold me here." I stand up. "I'd like to go."

"Sydney," Detective Lange says, standing as well. "If there's anything you aren't telling me, it's going to hurt you in the end. I suggest you be upfront with me now because while I don't have enough to hold you at this time, I'm going to dig into this and find what I need."

"Be my guest because whatever you find, isn't going to lead you to my front door. I didn't do anything but try to meet who I thought might be a great guy. So here's my official statement. I'm sorry I never got to know if Malcolm was the man I thought he was. I'm sorry I didn't get to see his reaction to me when we saw each other for the first time. And I'm sorry you have no clue who did this to him."

"Don't worry. I will find out who poisoned Malcolm Monaghan."

He doesn't seem to realize he slipped up and told me the cause of death. Of course, I'm sure it's not official since the coroner hasn't had time to examine the body yet. This has to mean they suspect it was the wine Malcolm was drinking. The wine he brought for us to share. I'm not sure what to make of that.

Chapter Three

I didn't feel any better when I woke up Saturday morning. For about thirty seconds, I contemplated if the whole ordeal had been an actual nightmare instead of one I'd lived through. But the memory of being in that interrogation room was way too real to pass off as a dream of any nature.

Knowing I'm not in the state of mind to sit through my morning sessions, I call Lena to cancel them. I don't book any in the afternoon on Saturdays. I allow myself a day and a half to enjoy the weekend. It's better for my patients anyway when I have the time I need to recharge.

"How did it go?" Lena asks.

"I guess you haven't watched the news."

"Your date was on the news?" she asks in a questioning tone.

"Unfortunately." I fill her in on what happened in the briefest manner possible.

"Oh, Sydney, I'm so sorry. I can't even imagine how awful that must have been for you."

"Yeah, well, I need to cancel today's sessions. I'm in no mood to help others right now."

"Of course. I'll take care of it for you. You take the time you need, and if there's anything else I can do, let me know."

"Thanks, Lena. You're the best." I hang up and dial Autumn as I sit down on the couch with my third cup of coffee of the morning.

"I was about to call you. I figured you slept in after your date."

I wish. I was up at four. "How was your night?" I ask her.

"Oh, no you don't. This conversation is about you and the potential Mr. Right."

Autumn never watches the news, so the fact that she has no idea Malcolm is dead doesn't surprise me.

"Are you sitting down?" I ask.

"Is it that good or that bad?" Her voice is laced with concern.

I dive into my Valentine's Day.

"I'm coming right over," Autumn says.

"Don't you have work today?" I hear the sound of keys jingling and know she's already in motion.

"I could ask you the same. The world is just going to have to get by without the two of us today." She really is the best friend ever.

She stays on the phone with me while she drives over. We don't talk much. It's more of a comfort thing, knowing she's there if I want to talk about it. I make some eggs and bacon, figuring she probably hasn't eaten yet. Autumn doesn't cook on weekends. She says she deserves two days off. She and Aaron usually go out for brunch.

"Did you even tell Aaron you were leaving?" I ask, plating the food.

"He was in the shower, so I texted him." I hear the sound of the engine cutting. "I'm here."

I end the call and open the front door. Autumn wraps me in a hug, and we stand in the doorway for a moment. "I'm okay. I didn't even really know him, so I can't be too broken up over it. I mostly feel awful that his life was taken when he was still so young."

She turns me around and shuts the door. Her nose twitches, and she guides me to the kitchen. "You were stress cooking."

I shrug. "I figured keeping busy is best."

She sits down, reaching for the glass of orange juice in front of her. "I agree, but keeping busy by figuring out who killed Malcolm and framed you is a better use of your time."

"I don't think I'm being framed. I'm not even sure who knew we were meeting in the park."

She starts eating and then points her fork at me. "After brunch, we need to dissect those emails you two sent each other. Maybe he mentioned something, and you missed it."

I nod. "I have no idea how to solve a murder. I don't even know the people in Malcolm's life, so how would I find out who had a reason to want him dead?"

Autumn bites her lower lip as she thinks. "All I know is Drew Lange is a jerk."

"He was doing his job. Of course, I'm also certain he was hoping to pin this on me and wrap up the case immediately."

"I'm sure his wife wasn't happy he missed most of Valentine's Day." Autumn smirks as she eats a slice of bacon.

"I might have said as much to him before I left the station." I still can't believe I did that, but he got me so angry.

Autumn laughs. "I wish I'd been there to see that."

"It was pretty amusing, but the bad part is I know he's going to look for a reason to haul me back to the station and pin this on me."

"But he won't find one. You had no reason to harm Malcolm. If anything, it was exactly the opposite. When Lange realizes how long it's been since you've had a date, he'll never believe you sabotaged your own chance at finding love."

"I think you're giving him too much credit." I don't know Andrew Lange well since he's about ten years older than I am. We were never in the same school. And my parents wouldn't know him either, so calling them in Florida now makes no sense at all. Besides, I don't want to worry them about this. If Mom hears I'm a suspect in a murder investigation, she'll hop on the first plane here, and then she'd probably assault Andrew Lange and get herself thrown in jail.

We finish eating and load the dishes into the dishwasher. Then we head to the living room, where I grab my laptop. For some reason, I hate emailing on my phone. I'm constantly hitting the wrong keys, and it frustrates me. I always tell my patients to avoid situations they know will upset them, and what kind of therapist would I be if I didn't follow my own advice?

I pull up my most recent email communication with Malcolm.

"No, start at the beginning," Autumn says. "I want to see exactly how everything unfolded."

I close the message and scroll back. I haven't cleared my inbox in a while, so all of our messages are still here.

"What about that?" Autumn asks, pointing to the same email Detective Lange was drawn to. The one where I complain about my job and say I'd like to teach one day. "Lange seems to think the job was the motivation for murder. What if he's right?"

I squint at the email as I reread it. "I think I see what you're saying. He mentions how things at the college aren't always great. That this Cohen guy is giving him a hard time and gunning for his course list."

Autumn bobs her head. "It sounds like he wanted Malcolm's job."

"You're right. But would this guy know about Malcolm's Valentine's Day plans with me?" I ask.

"Only one way to find out for sure."

The problem is it's Saturday, and the college isn't open for classes. I open a new tab in my browser and google First State College. It takes me a few minutes to locate the staff directory, but when I do, I scan the last names for Cohen.

"Gerard Cowen," I say as I open yet another tab in the browser to search for him.

"Hey, do you ever look up your patients like this?" Autumn asks.

I shake my head. "No. I don't really want to get an impression of them outside of my office. It might sway my opinion of them and change the way I communicate in our sessions. Plus, it would be an invasion of privacy."

Autumn furrows her brow. "If they're dumb enough to post something publicly online, that's on them. No invasion of privacy there."

"Yeah, but they trust me. If they find out I was snooping around online to get information, I'd break that trust and lose patients."

"Okay, so your moral compass is firmly intact. I get it. My job is different. The kids I see at the youth center know I'm watching them online. I tell them that if they post anything that would reflect badly on the youth center, I'll kick them out."

"Harsh."

"Tough love, baby. It works."

It must because I've seen Autumn with those teenagers, and they really respect her.

"So, according to his social media profiles, he lives here in town. It also says he used to work at the University of Delaware."

Autumn reads over my shoulder. "So he would definitely be bitter about going from a great school like that to a smaller college in a small town, right?"

"Unless he wanted a job closer to home," I say. "But we know he did want Malcolm's course load, and maybe this is why. Maybe he felt more qualified to teach the courses because he came from UD."

"That makes sense." She smiles at me. "You know, your background in psychology might make you a good detective. I bet you can find the killer before Detective Lange does."

"Let's hope so since he's not looking at anyone other than me at the moment."

"Do you want to go talk to Gerard Cowen?" she asks.

"I don't have any other plans for today."

We spend the next hour trying to find an address for Gerard. I'm not used to locating this kind of information on people. As it turns out, he was tagged in a photo online that had the location listed. That narrowed my search down enough to help me find his last known address. Autumn drives since her car is blocking mine in the driveway.

Gerard Cowen lives in a new housing development in Rehoboth Beach. The lots are small, but the houses are nice. Autumn pulls into the driveway and cuts the engine.

I can't tell if anyone is home. There doesn't appear to be a light on in the front of the house, but the home is deeper than it is wide, so it's possible Gerard is in one of the back rooms. We get out of the car and walk to the front door. I ring the doorbell and wait.

A yapping sound tells me Gerard owns a small dog. A deep voice tries unsuccessfully to hush the dog. Then the front door opens. Gerard is holding a breed I can't identify offhand.

"Yes?" He narrows his eyes at me and then Autumn.

"Are you Gerard Cowen?" I ask.

He bobs his head. "Who's asking?"

I didn't think about how I'd introduce myself. I barely knew Malcolm, but I'm going to have to pretend we were closer than we were if I want people to answer my questions. "I'm Sydney Warner. I was a friend of Malcolm Monaghan."

"Was?" he asks.

Seriously, does no one watch the news? "He was murdered last night."

Gerard stares blankly at me for a moment before bursting into a fit of laughter, which makes the dog squirm uncomfortably in his arms. He bends down to free the dog, who runs into another room. "Is this some sort of prank?"

"Who would joke about someone dying?" I ask him.

"Malcolm put you up to this, didn't he?" He crosses his arms. "He thinks he so funny. He tells me I'd get his classes over his dead body, and then he sends you to tell me he's dead."

"No, that's not what happened at all. Malcolm is dead. You can turn on the news and see for yourself if you'd like."

"Do you take me for a fool?" He lowers his arms, and his right hand curls into a fist.

"I don't even know you. If I'm being honest, I didn't know Malcolm very well either. I was supposed to meet him for our first date last night, but he was dead when I arrived."

Gerard studies me for a moment. "Are you being serious?"

"Mr. Cohen, we're both in the same field. If you're as good as I hear you claim to be, you should be able to tell if I'm being serious right now."

He accepts my challenge, like I knew he would. It was almost too easy. Textbook even. But then again, he's a professor, so it makes sense. "Okay, come in. I'd like to hear the news for myself."

"It's easier if you look it up online," Autumn tells him, and I'm grateful for it because I don't want to have to stand here while he watches an entire news segment to get to the part about Malcolm's passing.

He brings us to the living room in the back of the house and picks up an iPad from an end table beside a lounge chair. He taps the screen several times and then reads. "Well, I'll be. He really is dead."

I can't help noticing he doesn't seem upset about it. If it wasn't obvious that he didn't know about Malcolm's death before I arrived, I would suspect him right now. He didn't do this, though. He's just glad he'll benefit from it.

"So why are you here?" he asks me. "I wasn't exactly friends with Monaghan."

"But you worked with him. Did he happen to mention our date to anyone at the school?" I ask.

"He was bragging about it at lunch. I overheard him talking to some of our colleagues. He didn't get into details, though, which might have been my fault."

"Yours? What do you mean?"

Gerard puts the iPad down on the chair and faces me. "I might have asked him how his ex-wife feels about him dating a younger woman."

"I'm sorry, his what?" Are we talking about the same Malcolm Monaghan?

Gerard laughs. "He didn't tell you he was married before?"

I turn to Autumn, wondering what else Malcolm didn't tell me.

"I can't say I'm surprised. It was a nasty divorce."

"How so?" Autumn asks.

"Like I said, I wasn't friends with the man. But his ex-wife used to show up looking for him and his money."

"Was she angry?" If he wasn't paying alimony or something like that, it could have been a motive for murder.

"At first. But if you ask me, she was using that as a reason to come see him. I think she was still in love with him."

"Then why did they get divorced?" Autumn asks.

"The wife had an affair." His smile tells me he often threw that in Malcolm's face. I really don't care for Gerard Cowen, but I'm also starting to wonder if everything I thought I knew about Malcolm was actually a lie.

Chapter Four

Since Gerard doesn't know Malcolm's ex-wife's name, Autumn and I leave. I sit in the passenger seat, replaying all my interactions with Malcolm. He never once mentioned being married. I'm not sure why he'd keep it a secret. Maybe he was still upset that his wife had an affair. Maybe he still had feelings for her. I guess I'll never know because he can't answer any of my questions now.

Autumn drives to the deli on Main Street. The woman is always hungry. She can eat like a pig and never gain a pound, too. Sometimes I really hate her for that. If I so much as look at food, I have to hit the gym. Okay, it's not quite that bad, but I'd kill for her metabolism. She orders an everything bagel with turkey and swiss cheese and chipotle mayo. Did I mention she likes odd food combinations, too? The amount of meat on the bagel is enough to feed about three people and make each feel sufficiently full.

I order half a sandwich. Turkey on rye. No mayo. No cheese. I really need to start going to the gym more often so I can eat like a normal person. After grabbing our drinks, we take a seat at a table, and a girl brings us a bowl of pickles. Autumn and I always eat them separately even though you're really supposed to put them on your sandwich. We dig right in. Pickles might be the most perfect food on the planet in my opinion.

"Are you okay?" she asks me. "I know you weren't expecting to find out Malcolm was married."

"It's not like he was still married. It was over, right? I really shouldn't be upset about it."

"And what would you tell one of your patients who said that to you?"

I roll my eyes as I say, "You're entitled to your feelings, whatever they may be."

"So how do you really feel then?" she asks, popping another pickle slice into her mouth.

"He should have told me. I wouldn't have cared. But the fact that he kept it from me makes me question whether he didn't trust me not to run when he told me or if he wasn't sure it was really over with his wife and was dating me to find out how he felt."

Autumn dips her head to one side. "I didn't think of it that way, but it does make sense. I mean, she cheated, so it's not like he's the one who stopped loving her and asked for the divorce."

No, he got his heart stomped on. So maybe her coming to see him at the college all the time made him feel the need to test his own feelings. I might have only been in his life to serve that purpose. And maybe he did drink too much wine because he was having trouble dealing with his emotions last night. I have no idea what poison was in the wine or how much it would take to kill him, so I can't rule anything out.

The girl who makes the sandwiches walks over with a tray. She places our plates in front of us. "Can I get either of you anything else?"

"Only if you have a time machine I can borrow," I joke.

"Sorry, but the customer before you got the last one." Her joke surprises me, and I laugh.

"I needed that. Thanks."

"Enjoy your lunch."

Autumn digs right into hers, taking a bite so big I'm sure she'll start choking. "So good," she says with her mouth full.

"I wish I could make sense of some of this. I guess I was stupid for agreeing to meet a guy alone like that, and on Valentine's Day no less."

She puts her sandwich down. "Okay, so maybe it wasn't the most brilliant plan, but what thirty-year-old takes a chaperone on a date?"

"We could have double dated," I say.

"So it's my fault now?" she teases.

"Isn't everything?" I smile so she knows I'm kidding.

"You know what's going to happen, don't you?"

"What?" I bite into my sandwich, which is drier than dry without any mayo.

"When Detective Lange finds out Malcolm was married, he's going to assume you found out and murdered him."

I put down my sandwich, suddenly not hungry in the least anymore, if I ever was to begin with. "You're probably right. This is going to make me look worse than I already do."

"Do you think it's procedure to look into a victim's emails as quickly as Lange did?" she asks. "I mean that was lightning fast."

"I think he was hoping to be able to hold me at the station, but the question is, how did he get into the email? Wouldn't he need to contact next of kin or something?"

"Unless the email app was already open on Malcolm's phone. I'm sure he had it on him."

"He uses a generic passcode," I say. "He joked about it with me. It's the numbers one through seven in order."

"So if the police tried that and got right in, and he already had his email up…" She doesn't finish her statement.

"I'm starting to see why Drew Lange is so intent on pinning this on me. I can't even blame him. If I was really the last person to communicate with Malcolm, and he was meeting me, then I had means for sure."

"Whoa, that's my best friend you're building a case against. Knock it off. We both know you didn't do this. Besides, I was with you while you got ready. I'll be your alibi."

"Until the coroner comes up with time of death, I'm not sure that's going to help me. And everyone in this town knows you'd lie for me."

She bobs her head. "Of course, I would. Remember that time in the tenth grade, when you skipped first period, and I told Mr. Fischer you had female problems and were in the bathroom?"

I laugh. "He believed you because the idea of periods freaked him out so much he didn't want to discuss it any further."

"Yup. And no one was the wiser. You didn't get in trouble for cutting, and your parents never found out that you were with Tyler Graham."

"Tyler did get caught, though. His Spanish teacher wrote him up, and he got detention for it."

"We make a good team, Syd."

"Great, so how is this team of ours going to figure out who murdered Malcolm?"

"I say we go talk to his ex-wife. See if she held a grudge."

She's right. If this woman found out Malcolm was dating me, she could have flown off the handle and killed him. Of course, that would be stupid in hindsight since he was paying her alimony and that would stop when he died. Still, emotions win out over logic most of the time. I see it all too often. My patients will flat-out admit they know what they should do in a situation, but they can't do it because they're too upset to let something go.

"How do we find her?"

"Easy. We search marriage records."

"How do you know this?" I ask her.

She pulls out her phone. "I watch way too many true crime documentaries. It's like a sickness. They're very addicting."

"I'll take your word for it. Show me how this works." I scoot my chair around the table to see what she's doing on her phone.

She types in a search for marriage records. She enters Malcolm's name and finds what we're looking for. "Bingo! He married Sherry Armstead, though now she's Sherry Monaghan. She kept her married name after the divorce."

Did she do that because she still loved Malcolm? Or was it to avoid the paperwork and hassle of reverting to her maiden name?

"We'll need to do some digging to find her address. You want to stay here to research or go back to your place?"

I cock my head at her. "Are you avoiding your own home? You haven't called or texted Aaron once since I've seen you today. What's going on?"

She sighs. "Fine. We had a fight last night. I said we should have kids because I'm not getting any younger. He said we should wait a few years until we have more money saved up and finally have a house of our own."

I don't say I think he has a point there. Autumn always has my back, and if she wants kids, I'm not about to tell her she isn't thinking rationally. She's clearly thinking with her heart, and I can't fault her for that. I place my hand on hers. "Autumn, go home. I'm fine. Detective Lange hasn't tried to arrest me all day, so I must be in the clear."

She scoffs. "Sure."

"You shouldn't be here. You and Aaron need to talk. This is a big deal."

She takes another bite of her sandwich before wrapping up the rest. "Okay, but call me later. I want to know if you track down Sherry Monaghan. And don't even think about going to talk to her on your own. You don't know if she's a coldblooded killer. You need to be careful."

Even if she isn't a murderer, she probably won't be happy to see me at her doorstep if what Gerard Cowen said was true and she's still in love with Malcolm. She might even think I killed him.

"I promise I won't talk to her without you." I cross my heart with my index finger, something she and I have always done when making promises to each other.

She stands up. "All right, wish me luck."

"Good luck, and if you need backup, I'm only a phone call away."

She laughs as she walks out.

I finish eating and toss my garbage. Once I step outside, I realize my car isn't here. "Great." I pull out my phone and call for a ride. I really hate getting into cars with complete strangers, but it's too far to walk home. When Autumn realizes she left me stranded here, she's going to feel awful. I just hope she gets through making up with Aaron before the realization hits her. Knowing her, she'd turn around and try to come get me, putting off the necessary conversation with her husband in the process.

A black car pulls up, and the driver lowers the window. "Sydney Warner?" he asks.

"That's me." I get in the back seat and give him the address.

"Did you have a good Valentine's Day," he asks, trying to make small talk and having no idea what a loaded question that is.

"Sure," I say because I'm not about to lie across the back seat and open up to a total stranger.

"Glad to hear it. So many people hate the holiday. Me, I like the day-after sales. All the chocolate you can eat for half price." He laughs, and his shoulders bob up and down.

"That's me right there," I tell him, pointing to my house.

He pulls into the driveway, and I pay and tip him. "Have a good one," he says, after I get out of the car.

I start for the front door but don't even make it up the steps when a patrol car pulls into my driveway. "You've got to be kidding me," I say, unlocking my door. I step inside, pretending I don't notice Detective Lange at all, and lock the door behind me.

I know I can't ignore him when he rings the bell, but at least I'll have a few seconds to regain my composure before I have to speak to him again.

I take off my jacket and hang it up in the hall closet. Then I put on the teakettle. I'm usually a coffee drinker, but I'm pretty sure I remember Detective Lange ordering tea the last time we were both inside the café.

The doorbell rings, and I call, "Just a minute." I turn on the burner on the stove before going to the door. I pull it open. "Detective, what brings you here?"

"I have a few more questions for you, Sydney. May I come in, or would you rather do this down at the station?" His choice of words doesn't elude me. He's letting me know he's doing me a favor by coming to me instead of bringing me downtown.

"Come right in. I just put on a pot of tea if you're interested."

"I'd love a cup. Thank you." He follows me to the kitchen, his gaze taking in the interior of my house on the way. "You've redecorated."

"I wasn't aware you were ever inside my grandmother's house," I say.

"Only a few times. When I was in high school, I cut her lawn for her."

"You did?" I grab two mugs from the cabinet above the counter.

He nods. "For three summers in a row. She'd always offer me lemonade and cookies. Sometimes, when it was really hot out, she'd tell me to come inside and cool off for a bit between mowing the front and back yards. She was a nice woman."

"She was," I say.

"It was nice what you did for her."

I was the only family she had left in Swan Creek. Mom and Dad had already moved to Florida, and I knew it would kill Dad to watch his mother deteriorate the way she did. My mom's mom had passed a few years before, and she still hadn't fully recovered from that. I always thought it was cruel the way kids have to watch their parents slowly drift away in their final days. I was happy to spare my parents from having to go through it again, and truth be told, I think it actually helped my grandmother having me here. She always told me I was her favorite. I was also her only grandchild, but still.

I clear my throat as the teakettle whistles on the stove. To my surprise, Detective Lange beats me to it, pulling it off the hot burner. "Thank you." I take it from him and pour the hot liquid into the mugs. I bring them to the table before getting my grandmother's tea box. She'd had it for as long as I could remember. "I have green tea, black, herbal, and chamomile. Take your pick." I open the box and place it on the table in front of Detective Lange.

He selects a tea bag and dunks it into his mug. "Thank you. Sydney, I'm sorry to have to ask you this, but you have to understand that the circumstances under which Malcolm Monaghan died do seem suspicious."

"Isn't murder always suspicious?" I ask, sitting down beside him.

He dips his head. "I suppose so, yes. But I mean the suspicion seems to consistently point to you."

"I know being the one to find the body makes me look guilty."

"Not to mention he was meeting you there."

"I have an alibi. Does that help?"

He bobs his head. "Yes, actually. Who is it?" He pulls a pad and pen from an inside pocket of his jacket.

"Autumn Young. She's my best friend, and she came over to help me get ready for my date."

"What time did you leave Autumn?"

"I think it was about a quarter to eight."

"I see."

"Do you know time of death?" I ask.

"I'm afraid I can't give you that information, Dr. Warner."

My head jerks back. "Dr. Warner? What happen to calling me Sydney?" This is a classic case of distancing himself from me so he doesn't feel guilty for making these accusations.

"I'm sorry. The hardest part of being a detective in a small town like this is I know almost everyone who lives here."

"Did you know Malcolm?" I ask.

"I only knew of him. Kind of like how I knew of you before all this."

Ah, so in other words, he and I aren't friends, and he's not going to do me any favors. "Detective Lange, you knew my grandmother. Do you think someone related to her would be capable of murder?"

"Your grandmother was an extraordinary woman, and I'm very sorry that she's no longer with us, but this isn't about her. I have a case to solve. Your alibi still puts you at the scene of the crime with plenty of time to have committed the murder. I'm sorry."

"But you have no proof."

"You're right. But you also know my job requires me to keep searching for some."

"Go right ahead. Search my house if you'd like. I have nothing to hide."

He cocks his head. "You're giving me permission to search your home?"

What am I doing? He's going to look for anything and everything to use against me, but I can't say no now, or I'll look guilty.

"That's what I said." I swallow hard and hope I didn't just make a huge mistake.

Chapter Five

Detective Lange finishes his tea so fast I'm not sure how he doesn't scald his mouth. Then he stands up, brings his mug to the sink, and says, "I'd like to start with your bedroom."

He's really going to do this. I get up and walk him to the bedroom. I immediately open my underwear drawer. "I'd prefer if you didn't root around in here, so look." I remove the drawer and dump the contents on my bed.

Satisfied there's nothing for him to find in there, he nods and begins opening other drawers while I put this one back together. It's hard to watch him go through all my things, so I go back to the kitchen and text Autumn to tell her what's going on."

My phone rings almost immediately. "What do you mean you told him he can search your house? Are you crazy?"

"Apparently, yes." I sit down at the table. "But it's not like he's going to find anything, so this is good, right? It will clear my name."

"Maybe. Do you want me to come over?"

"No. I didn't even expect you to call me. You and Aaron are supposed to be talking."

"This isn't an issue we're going to solve in a day. I've said my peace. We both need time to think over the other's argument right now. I'll be there in ten minutes."

"Okay." I end the call and place the phone beside my mug, slightly relieved that Autumn is on her way to help me through this.

I can hear drawers closing in the bedroom every few minutes. Detective Lange is being very thorough, which will hopefully mean this will all be over once he leaves.

There's a knock on my front door, and then it opens. I get up to meet Autumn in the entryway. She wraps me in a hug before saying, "Where is he?"

"My bedroom."

She nods once and marches in that direction with me following. "Detective," she says, entering the room.

He turns around to face her.

"This is my best friend, Autumn Young," I tell him.

"Her alibi," Autumn adds.

"I'm aware you were with Sydney before she left to meet the victim at the park. Unfortunately, that doesn't get her off the hook because she still could have committed the murder."

"If the time of death was so close to when Sydney arrived, wouldn't someone at the park have seen the killer?" Autumn asks him.

"Most likely, yes. But a lot of people go to that park. The bench was concealed by the willow tree, so it's possible no one was seen under the branches with Malcolm, but they could have been seen elsewhere," Detective Lange says, his gaze on me.

"If he left from the back of the tree, he could have gone into the woods without being seen," I say. Other than the pathway looping around the park, there's nothing but trees on that side of the willow tree. If no one was on that part of the path, the killer could have gotten away unseen.

"He?" Detective Lange asks. "What makes you think the killer is a man?"

"I can't say for sure, obviously."

"Right, just like you can't say for sure it's Sydney," Autumn offers, crossing her arms in front of her.

"It's probably best that you two go in another room while I continue my search."

"What exactly are you looking for?" Autumn asks.

Detective Lange already has the emails Malcolm and I sent each other. He can get Malcolm's phone records as well. That would leave whatever poison was used to kill him. I'm surprised he's not in my bathroom, thinking that's where he'd find such a thing.

"I understand this isn't easy, but I'm doing my job. A man was murdered. I have to do everything in my power to find out why and by whom." His tone is level, almost devoid of emotion.

I tug on Autumn's elbow. "Come on. I have a kettle of hot water in the kitchen."

"I think we both could use a stiff drink, not tea." She follows me out of the room, but not before glaring at Detective Lange one more time. "You know it's people like him who give cops a bad name," she says loudly enough for Detective Lange to hear. "I mean, you reported the murder, and instead of thanking you, he's accusing you. You're an innocent bystander. No, you're a victim. Malcolm could have been your future husband for all we know."

I'm not sure about that. Malcolm was clearly keeping secrets. Not that he owed me an explanation since we'd only just met, but I can't help thinking there's a reason he didn't tell me he was previously married.

"Can we talk about something else?" I say, grabbing a margarita in a bottle from the refrigerator and handing it to her.

"What is this?" she eyes the ridiculously small bottle.

"Cute, right? I saw them at the store and thought of you."

"Hey." Autumn is only five foot one, and she's a little sensitive about her height.

"Not because of the size." I laugh. "I mean because you love margaritas but hate going through the effort to make them. This is ready to go."

"Oh. Why is it so small? And I feel I can ask that considering I'm smaller than most people."

"They're mini bottles. I think they're adorable."

She twists the top off and takes a sip. "Not bad."

Footsteps alert me that Detective Lange is finished in my bedroom. He walks into the living room and begins removing the couch cushions.

"Make sure you put everything back where you found it," Autumn tells him. "If you ask me, Sydney is being way too cooperative about all this."

He doesn't respond, but he does return each cushion to its proper place, so I guess that's something.

"I'm starting to hate Valentine's Day," Autumn says. "Aaron and I got into a fight, and you found your date murdered in the park. I think that calls for officially canceling the holiday for all future years."

"I agree," I say, raising my mug and clinking it against her bottle.

Autumn leans toward me and whispers, "Does Detective Lange know about the ex-wife?"

I shrug. "He said he had some questions for me, but we wound up talking about my grandmother, and then I stupidly told him he could search the place, so he never actually asked me anything. He only said all the clues were pointing in my direction."

She bites her bottom lip as she thinks. "Hmm. He might not have anything then. He could have been trying to set you up. You know, make you think he knew something in hopes that you'd accidentally give up some useful information."

She might be right about that. I mean what does he think he'll find in my living room? Unless he thinks I hid a bottle of poison in my couch. Would anyone be stupid enough to do that?

I wish my laptop wasn't still in the living room. I could be doing something useful, like looking up Sherry Monaghan's address. I need to talk to her. If she's as unhinged as Gerard Cowen made her out to be, she could be the killer. Showing up at Malcolm's place of work without an invitation could have led to following him on our date last night. She could have acted out in rage.

No. Poison would need to be planned for. This murder was premeditated. But maybe she found out about our date and decided to put an end to it before it even began.

It's the best theory I can come up with at the moment. I grab my phone from the table and start searching. I turn the screen to Autumn so she can see what I'm doing. After a curt nod, she grabs her phone and does the same.

There's one listing in Swan Creek for Sherry Monaghan. I type the address into my navigation app. She lives eight minutes away from me. If Detective Lange finishes up soon, I could be at Sherry's house in no time and maybe get the answers I need.

I show Autumn my phone, and she gives me a thumbs-up.

"Where did Detective Lange go?" she whispers to me.

"I don't know. Maybe the guest bedroom." I use the space as a library since I never have guests stay the night. There is a pullout couch though if the occasion ever did arise.

We stand up to go see.

"Detective?" I call before entering the room.

The bathroom door opens, making me jump. I press my hand to my chest. "You scared me!"

"Why are you so jumpy?" Detective Lange asks.

"Gee, I wonder," Autumn says. "Could it be that you're accusing her of murdering someone she barely knew, and now you're searching her home for evidence to lock her up?"

I grab Autumn's forearm. She's not the type to let anyone push her or her loved ones around, and one of these days she's going to say the wrong thing to the wrong person and get herself in a lot of trouble. I'm hoping that day isn't today.

"Why is the vanity practically empty in there?" Detective Lange asks, jerking his thumb over his shoulder.

"I never use that bathroom. It's more of a guest bathroom, and I don't have many guests."

"You didn't recently dispose of anything from that room?"

"Would you like to check my garbage?" I ask, unable to comprehend how much this man doesn't believe a word I say.

"Actually, yes." He pulls a latex glove from inside his jacket.

"You've got to be kidding me," Autumn says.

"Not even a little bit." He holds out his arm, motioning for me to lead the way.

I roll my eyes and bring him to the garage. I point to the large gray trash can. "Have fun."

He levels me with a look before walking past me and opening the lid. He grabs the bag on top and unties it.

"Careful, there's old Chinese food in there," I warn him. "I'm sure it stinks by now."

"Why'd you order so much?" he asks me. "Were you expecting company?"

"No, I tried something new but didn't like it, so I threw it out."

"Uh-huh." He continues to rifle through the trash.

"Why does it seem like you've done this before?" Autumn asks. "You're very at home in the garbage."

She is really asking to be handcuffed at this point. "Autumn, come on. Let's let Detective Lange do his job."

"Hang on," he says, returning the bag to the trash can and then removing his glove and tossing that in as well. "I think I'm finished here. Do you have an attic or basement?"

"My attic is a crawlspace. You can't even stand up in it."

"And the basement?"

I nod and motion for him to follow me. I bring him to the door beside the hall closet and open it. "Down there."

"Are you sure you don't want to sell me this house?" Autumn asks. "It would solve two of my current problems, my living arrangements and a place to raise a child."

"Did you imply you'd raise your child in the basement?" Detective Lange asks, his brow furrowed.

"No, that's not what I was saying. And I was talking to Sydney, not you. She knows what I meant."

I do, but I have to admit Detective Lange has a point. It did sound like she was saying she'd stick her child in the basement. Of course, I know she's looking for a house with a basement because that's what Aaron wants, and he wants to be settled in a home before they have children.

Detective Lange shakes his head before flipping the light switch and heading down the stairs.

"Do you want to follow him down?" Autumn asks me.

"No, I never go in the basement. It's so musty smelling. My grandmother has a wine cellar down there and not much else."

"I can't believe there's wine in your basement, and you've been holding out on me."

"You're not even a big wine drinker," I say.

"Still. She might have some good stuff. You could probably sell it."

Detective Lange is heading back upstairs already.

"I guess the place is small if he's finished already," Autumn says.

"Care to explain this?" Detective Lange asks, holding a bottle of wine out toward me.

"What?" I ask.

"This happens to be a bottle of Domaine Leroy Musigny Grand Cru 2012."

"I have no idea what that means. That wine belonged to my grandmother. She was a collector. I don't even drink the stuff."

"Really?" Detective Lange asks. "Then why did Malcolm Monaghan have a bottle of this on him at the park? The very same bottle that contained the poison that killed him?"

"I don't know. I guess it's a popular wine." I shrug.

"Oh, it's popular because of the fact that it's rare, vintage, and quite costly." He spins the bottle around to read the label. "This particular vintage costs about fifteen thousand dollars a bottle."

"What?" Autumn grabs my arm so tightly I'm sure she's leaving finger imprints on my skin. "Syd, you could be sitting on a gold mine down there."

"I had no idea. Grandma Warner never mentioned that any of the wine was rare or vintage."

"More importantly, the spot next to this bottle in the wine rack is empty," Detective Lange says.

"So?" I ask.

"So, it seems to me that it probably contained another bottle of Domaine Leroy Musigny Grand Cru 2012 at one time," he says.

I shake my head. "You just said it's rare and very expensive. Why would my grandmother have two bottles of the stuff?"

"That's a question you're going to need to answer down at the station," he says.

"What? You can't be serious."

"I'm afraid I am. Sydney, you need to come with me, and I suggest you come willingly."

"Do I need a lawyer?" I ask Autumn.

"I'll call one and meet you there."

I have no idea what's happening, but I'm suddenly feeling like this bottle of wine is going to land me in prison.

Chapter Six

The lawyer Autumn calls for me actually beats us to the station. I have no idea how, but she does. And she's as intimidating as a grizzly bear. She's about six feet tall, giving her two inches or so on Detective Lange even in flats. Her dark hair is pulled back in a sleek updo, and a black power suit and briefcase complete the look.

"Detective, what charges are you pressing against my client?" she asks in a no-nonsense manner.

"I'm not charging her yet, Ms. Overthorn," he says, walking past her to the interrogation room. "In here please."

I step inside, not sure if I'm supposed to introduce myself to this lawyer. She clearly knows who I am, which means Autumn filled her in on the phone, but I don't even know the woman's full name.

"Ms. Overthorn, I'm aware of your reputation," Detective Lange begins.

"Good, then let's cut to the chase. Unless you have concrete evidence to hold my client, I'd like it acknowledged that she is here of her own free will and cooperating fully with your investigation."

Detective Lange bobs his head. "Duly noted."

"Wait, I don't have to be here?" I ask.

"Take a seat, Sydney," Ms. Overthorn says, and the way she points to the chair makes me feel like I was called into the principal's office to be reprimanded.

I sit down. "Would someone please tell me what's going on?"

Detective Lange places the bottle of wine on the table. "This is an exact match to the bottle of wine at the crime scene."

"You mean it matches the bottle that Malcolm brought to the park," I say.

"So you say."

"So said Malcolm in his email to me. You read them. You should know this."

"What email?" my lawyer asks.

I grab my phone and find the conversation. "There. Malcolm says he's bringing the dinner and the wine. I only needed to show up. I didn't have any wine on me. You can ask the woman whose dog I stopped from running away. She saw me."

"What's the woman's name?" Detective Lange asks me.

"I don't know. I've never met her before."

"Can you describe her?" he asks, letting out a huff of air.

"She was small. Blond, curly hair."

"Anything else? Distinguishing features, like a birthmark or tattoo?"

"None that I saw. It was dark, and I was a little too busy catching the dog to pay much attention to the woman. Besides, you can ask Autumn to confirm that I didn't bring a bottle of wine with me to the park. She saw me."

"And she's your best friend," Detective Lange says, dismissing Autumn as a reliable witness.

"Detective, it is not my client's job to find this woman with the dog or anyone else who saw Sydney without the wine that night. It's yours. Now, do you have any other questions?" Ms. Overthorn says.

"Yes." Detective Lange clears his throat.

"Well?" Ms. Overthorn waves her hand at him. "Ask."

He looks at me. "How do you explain having the same bottle of wine in the basement?"

"I can't. It was my grandmother's, like I said. I didn't even know it was there. I only knew she had a wine cellar. I don't know the first thing about wine. Believe me, if I'd known how much that bottle was worth, I would have sold it."

"Are you sure you didn't sell it to Malcolm Monaghan?" he asks. "You had two bottles after all. Why not sell one?"

"I didn't sell any wine."

"How do you explain the missing bottle then?"

"I can't. How do you even know it was missing? Maybe there never was a bottle there."

"Easy. The amount of dust or lack of dust in that particular spot tells me someone recently removed a bottle."

"No one has been down there. I don't even use the basement."

Ms. Overthorn holds up a hand to stop me. "My client has nothing further to say on the matter. Any other questions?"

Detective Lange's gaze bores into mine. "Sydney, I'm going to prove this bottle had a companion in your basement wine cellar. I can assure you of that."

"We're finished here, Detective. Sydney, let's go," Ms. Overthorn says.

I get to my feet and follow her out. I'm not sure who I'm more afraid of right now, her or the detective trying to put me behind bars for a murder I didn't commit. I follow her out of the station to her car.

"Here's my card." She hands me a business card. "If Detective Lange contacts you again, call me immediately. Do not say a word to him without me present. Do you understand?"

"Yes."

"Good." She gets in her car and drives away.

Once again, I have no ride. This time I call Autumn.

"Are you okay?" she answers.

"As okay as I can be given the circumstances, but now I'm stranded at the police station without a ride home."

"I'll be right there. Did Norelle beat you to the station?"

Norelle? Even her first name sounds intense. It's like her parents knew she'd become a cutthroat lawyer when she was still in the womb. "Yeah, she was here. She wouldn't let Detective Lange say much. It felt more like she was running the interrogation than he was."

"Good. That's how it should be. He has no proof."

"He's sure there was another bottle of that wine missing from the rack."

"But again, he can't prove it. He's got nothing on you but circumstantial evidence. He can't make any charges stick, and he knows it. That's why he's so cranky."

"The weird thing is he knew my grandmother. He even liked her. Yet here he is thinking her granddaughter is capable of murder." I start walking toward the road, wanting to put distance between me and Detective Lange. I stop at the intersection and look back at the station. Detective Lange walks outside and gets in his patrol car.

"He's leaving again," I tell Autumn, who's been talking even though I didn't listen to a word she said.

"See which direction he goes in. Maybe we can figure out what he's up to."

I turn away from his car as he pulls out of the parking lot, but I use my peripheral vision to watch him. "He's coming toward me."

"Do not talk to him," she says.

"You sound like Overthorn."

"Yeah, well, she's right. Listen to her. She'll chew up Lange and spit him out."

The light turns red, and Detective Lange stops at the intersection. His gaze lands on me.

"He's looking right at me."

"Whatever you do, don't look guilty. You've done nothing wrong, Syd."

"I know that, but I can't help feeling like a criminal when I'm being treated like one." I pretend to pick a piece of lint off my jacket.

The light changes, and Detective Lange drives straight through it. "He's gone," I tell Autumn.

"Good. Any idea to where?"

"Maybe to see Sherry Monaghan. That road would take him to the part of town where she lives."

"He does know about her then. Okay, that's good. Hopefully, she'll create some suspicion when he questions her. I'm five minutes away. Just hang tight."

"Autumn, remind me to never date again when this is all over."

"I'm sorry. I'm the one who made you sign up for Kindred Hearts to begin with. This is all my fault."

"No, it's not. There's no way you could have known this would happen."

"Yeah, but I shouldn't have pushed you to talk to a complete stranger. I just want you to be happy."

"I know you do, and I love you for that. And thank you for calling Overthorn. She's scary intimidating."

"No problem. I met her in college. She owed me a favor, so I thought I'd cash in. She's the type that hates to lose, so she's a bit over-the-top when it comes to intimidation. I'm sure she broke every speed limit to beat you guys to the station so she could one-up Detective Lange at getting to the interrogation as well."

"I'm guessing you didn't meet her at a frat party," I joke.

She laughs. "No, I wound up taking a law class as an undergrad. I might have been slightly tipsy when I registered for my courses that semester, and the professor wouldn't let me drop the class without it going on my record, so I stuck it out. Hated every second of it, but I met Norelle, and we've been friends ever since. Well, as much of friends as you can be when one of you has zero social life. I basically refer clients to her. She helped me out once, too, when my cousin tried to dispute our grandfather's will."

I see her car pull up to the intersection, and I jog over, getting into the passenger seat. "Thanks."

"Any time." The light is red, so she turns to me. "What do you want to do now?"

I could go home and wallow in a pint of cookie dough, a plan I do like the sound of, or I could go see Sherry Monaghan. "Detective Lange is probably at Sherry's house."

"Let's find out," Autumn says. "We can stake out the house from down the street."

"He knows your car now. You had to let him out of my driveway about an hour ago, remember?"

"I drive a gray Honda Civic, which is about the most common car there is. I can make sure we blend in." The light changes, and she drives straight.

I still have Sherry's address in my navigation app, so I give Autumn the directions. Detective Lange's patrol car is still parked in front of her house when we arrive. Autumn pulls past the house and parks around the corner. There's a big bush on the corner of the property we're parked in front of, so hopefully the car is pretty well concealed. We should still be able to see when Detective Lange leaves, though.

"How great would it be if he walks out of there with Sherry in handcuffs?" Autumn says.

"You're quite the optimist today," I say.

"I figure the universe owes you." She keeps her gaze trained on the patrol car.

"How long have Sherry and Malcolm been divorced?" she asks me.

"About a year now. Why?"

"Well, didn't Gerard Cowen say she was angry with Malcolm at first, but then she changed? Maybe she decided she wasn't over him, and that's why she started coming around again, to work things out. But Malcolm had already moved on. To you."

"Hardly. We hadn't even met in person."

"Maybe not, but if she was snooping around in his personal life, she could have known about you. That you two were talking. And she could have looked you up like we looked her up."

"What are you saying?"

"I'm saying she might know a lot more about you than we think. Even that you live in your grandmother's house and that your grandmother was a wine collector."

"Do you think she followed me home and broke into my basement to steal a bottle of my grandmother's wine?" I ask, scoffing at the absurdity.

"Do you have a better explanation?" She widens her eyes at me.

No, but if she did know there was expensive rare wine in my basement, why wouldn't she sell the bottle and keep the money? Was killing Malcolm worth more to her than the money?

Chapter Seven

About thirty minutes later, Detective Lange gets in his patrol car and drives right toward us.

"Get down," Autumn says, slouching down in her seat as far as possible.

I do the same, hoping Detective Lange didn't get a good look at Autumn's license plate back at my house. The last thing I need is for him to realize we followed him, even though we were planning to come here anyway.

"Is he gone?" Autumn asks.

"I don't know. He should be, unless he recognized your car and stopped to see what we'd do."

"Well, we can't stay like this all evening. Not to mention it's nearly dinnertime. Aaron's probably making kabobs as we speak."

Yum. If they weren't working through the whole baby and house buying thing, I'd invite myself over for dinner. I slowly sit up in my seat and peek out the window. "I don't see the patrol car. I think it's safe."

Autumn sits up and pulls the car around to Sherry's house. She doesn't pull into the driveway, opting to park out front instead. I can't help thinking it's in case Detective Lange returns. He wouldn't be able to block her car in this way.

We get out and walk up to the front door. Autumn rings the bell.

A woman opens the door. She's pretty, and I feel a slight pang of jealousy, which is ridiculous since Malcolm is dead, and there's no chance of me winding up with him.

"Sherry Monaghan?" I ask.

"Yes?" A flicker of recognition crosses her face, making me think Autumn was right. Sherry does know who I am.

"You know me, don't you?" I ask. "I mean you know of me."

She sighs. "You found his body, didn't you?"

I nod. "May we come in?"

She steps aside. "Sure. I have some questions for you as well."

I step into the house, which is really nicely decorated and pristine. "You have a lovely home," I say.

"Thank you. My boyfriend would disagree with you." There's bitterness in her tone.

If she's dating someone else, why was she showing up at the college to see Malcolm? Maybe Gerard Cowen was wrong. Maybe Sherry really didn't like Malcolm. But did she hate him enough to kill him?

"Why doesn't he like it?" Autumn asks. "It's beautiful."

"He wants me to move. He says I should cut all ties to my previous marriage, but I don't see the point in selling a great house like this."

"Do you have a basement?" Autumn asks, and I can tell she's mentally picturing her own furniture in this place.

I smack her arm. This is not the time to be house hunting.

"I do," Sherry says. "It runs the full length of the house, too. Jared uses it as his home office. He likes complete quiet when he works." She rolls her eyes. "He's a theoretical chemist at a lab in Dover."

"Is he at work now?" I ask.

"Yeah, he's usually home by seven. The commute can be killer sometimes." She motions to the kitchen. "Can I offer either of you a drink?"

"No, thank you." Considering Malcolm was poisoned, I'm not about to drink anything she offers me.

"I'm good," Autumn says, following my lead.

We all sit down at the kitchen table.

"So, you were dating Malcolm," Sherry says to me.

"Hardly. It was supposed to be our first date."

"On Valentine's Day?" she asks. "That's putting a lot of pressure on the relationship, don't you think?"

"It was supposed to be very casual, hence meeting at the park." I lace my fingers in my lap and stare at them, not wanting to look Sherry in the eyes. "Can I ask you about the divorce?"

She laughs. "I should've expected that question, I suppose." She stands up and opens the refrigerator, removing a bottle of Coke. "I had an affair."

I'm kind of surprised she admits to it so easily. "With the man you're currently living with?"

"Jared, yes. I'm sure you're judging me, but Malcolm was not an easy man to be married to. Do you have any idea what it's like having the person you live with dissecting your every thought and action?"

Clearly, she didn't look into me too much or she'd know I'm a psychologist. "I think I can imagine."

She laughs. "Oh, that's right. That's probably what drew you two together, huh?"

Okay, so she does know. "It was nice having someone understand what it's like. It's hard not to read into people's actions when the reasoning behind them is so obvious to us."

"Why do I feel like this is going to turn into a free therapy session? Or should I get my checkbook?" She raises one eyebrow in challenge.

"Nothing like that. I'm trying to understand what happened to Malcolm. Did he mention our date to you?"

She sits up straighter. "Are you accusing me of something?"

"No. Not at all. I'm merely curious if he made the date known to those around him. If a lot of people knew about it, it would make it easier for someone to kill him."

"Well, I didn't know about it. I mean I knew he had plans, and I did know they were with you, but I didn't know the location."

"Were you upset that Malcolm was dating?" Autumn asks. "I'm guessing not since you're with your boyfriend now."

"Jared is nothing like Malcolm. They're polar opposites." The way she says it doesn't imply if that's a good thing or a bad thing. If Malcolm was always analyzing everything she did, did that mean Jared didn't understand why she did things? I could see how that might be equally as annoying.

"Mrs. Monaghan, if Malcolm knew you so well, didn't he at least suspect you were having an affair?" I ask. It seems to me that she wouldn't be able to get something like that past him.

"Oh yes, he knew. He told me I did it to get his attention." She flips a hand in the air. "He was always working, whether it was teaching classes or writing scholarly papers. He wanted to publish books with his findings. I swear it boosted his ego every time one of his articles got published." She smiles. "I took it almost as a challenge."

"What? Trying to see how long you could cheat on him without him finding out?" I ask.

She shrugs. "By that point, it was clear he loved his work more than he loved me, so what did I really have to lose?"

She got the house in the divorce as well as alimony, so I'd say she did pretty well for herself. "How long before he found out?"

"Two months. Though he claims he knew from the start but debated the nastiness of going through with divorce proceedings. As if I believed that for a second."

"Did you stop loving him?" I need to know because it's the only way to know if what Gerard Cowen perceived as Sherry wanting Malcolm back was true.

"I stopped being content being his second love. Let's leave it at that."

That's not exactly the same as saying she fell out of love. So maybe Gerard was right. "Why did you go see Malcolm at the college? You've clearly moved on." I gesture to the house, though I'm actually inclined to side with Sherry's new man, Jared, on this one. Staying in the house she and Malcolm bought together is a clear sign that she's trying to hold on to what they had. She can't be keeping it for the money, because it's a seller's market right now, and this place would sell in a heartbeat.

"He was late with a few alimony checks."

Another thought strikes me. If she's been with Jared for over a year, why haven't they discussed marriage? Could it be because she still loved Malcolm? She might have been using the alimony checks as a reason to delay getting married. It would seem like a plausible excuse if she did need the money. "I see. Are you currently out of work?"

"No. I'm an administrative assistant. I make good money because I've been with the company since I was twenty-five." I'm guessing she's the same age as Malcolm, so that means she's been with the company for almost ten years now.

"Oh, then was hounding him for the alimony checks actually about the divorce and not the money itself?" I don't mean for it to come out as harshly as it does. "Sorry, that wording wasn't quite right."

She cocks her head at me. "Are you questioning how I was able to get him to pay alimony when I cheated?"

Kind of, yeah. It doesn't make much sense to me. "Sorry, I don't mean to pry. It's just that I'm not familiar with the process at all. I don't know how it works."

"And we're assuming you cheated for good reason," Autumn throws in. She's still taking in the house like she's going to be living here one day, and I suspect she wants to suck up to Sherry to help that dream become a reality.

"I did have a good reason. I already told you what it was. Do you know what it's like to not be appreciated? He took me for granted. If you ask me, you dodged a bullet," she says, addressing me. But her bottom lip quivers slightly, giving away her true feelings. She's upset Malcolm is dead.

"I'm sure it was very difficult for you. I know what it's like to be hurt by someone you love." It's been a long time, but I've had my heart broken before. I'm hoping since I can relate to her feelings, I'll be able to get her to open up to me. I feel a little guilty doing this since I'm playing her and using her feelings to manipulate her, but what else am I supposed to do when I'm trying to clear my own name?

"Then you know the pain."

I nod. "You know what I think the worst part is?" The next part is really hard to get out because I'm going against everything I believe in as a therapist manipulating her like this. "Still loving them when you know you shouldn't because they don't deserve your love."

"Yes!" She stands up. "You do get it."

I nod again and look away, pretending to be lost in my own emotions. Really my guilty conscience is screaming at me to show some professionalism.

Autumn gives me the side eye and then says, "I think I know what you mean. It's tough because the heart isn't always rational. It refuses to listen to our brains when we tell it to run far away. I tried to get back together with an ex once." She huffs. "Awful guy. Truly awful. But I loved him." She bobs a shoulder, and I'm really impressed with her performance because I know that was all a lie she just made up off the top of her head when she realized what I was doing.

"Men, am I right?" Sherry asks.

"So right," Autumn says. "Honestly, I'm not sure how you stay here. I mean, yes, the house is gorgeous, but it must hold so many painful memories."

Oh boy. I need to step in before she throws an offer out for Sherry's house and ruins everything. "Sherry, I wanted to offer my condolences and tell you that despite what you might hear, Malcolm was already dead when I found him at the park. I didn't see anyone. I thought maybe you'd have an idea who might want to hurt him since you knew him so much better than I did."

"I might have a few ideas." She holds up a finger and nods. "His coworker Gerard Cowen."

"I suspected him, too," Autumn says. She motions back and forth between them. "We are on the same wavelength. It's uncanny."

I resist the urge to roll my eyes at her.

"We talked to Gerard. He actually pointed the finger at you," I say.

"Which is ludicrous," Autumn says. "Obviously."

I may need to muzzle her. "Can you think of anyone else?" I ask.

Sherry nods. "His neighbor. A real viper of a woman. She's had her eye on Malcolm since the day he moved in."

"What's her name?" I ask, pulling out my phone to jot the name in my notes app.

"Rochelle Howey. She's twenty-eight and looking for a man to support her. She was always throwing herself at Malcolm. It was embarrassing. I feel sorry for her, but maybe she got tired of him rejecting her and took matters into her own hands."

"Do you think she would have known about my date with Malcolm?" I ask.

"She very well could have. She kept a close eye on him. I'm sure she knew whenever he left the house. I wouldn't even be surprised if she followed him, found out he planned a romantic meeting with another woman, and killed him on the spot."

The problem with that plan is that the murder was definitely premeditated. If Malcolm had been hit over the head or strangled, I'd say Sherry was probably on to something. But it is possible that this Rochelle found out about the date ahead of time and planned the murder from there. She might have even intended to frame me since she probably viewed me as the obstacle in her way to getting the man of her dreams.

I jot down Rochelle's name. I know where Malcolm lives because he told me in an email. I feel a little bad that I didn't trust him with my address, but I still don't have a firm grasp on what kind of man Malcolm truly was, so maybe I was right to be careful with my personal information.

The front door opens, and we all turn in that direction.

"In here, Jared," Sherry calls.

A tall man with glasses and dirty blond hair walks into the kitchen. "Who's this?" he asks Sherry, bending down to kiss her hello.

"Jared, this is…" Sherry pauses and looks at Autumn and me. "I'm sorry, but I've forgotten your names."

"I'm Sydney Warner. This is Autumn Young. We just wanted to talk to Sherry about Malcolm Monaghan."

"Why?" Jared asks. "She divorced him."

"We know, but he died last night."

"I don't see how that's any concern of Sherry's."

I stand up. "Okay, well, we should get going. Thank you for your time, Sherry."

Autumn follows my lead. We exit the house and get into her car. "That was weird, right?" she asks me once we're back on the road.

"Very. Sherry still has feelings for Malcolm. Or she did at least. That much is clear."

"But Jared doesn't seem to know about that."

Which is probably a good thing. I doubt he'd stick around with a woman who was still in love with her ex. "What's really strange is that Sherry cheated on Malcolm with Jared and then snuck out to go see Malcolm behind Jared's back."

"Yeah, that's messed up. She's a strange woman for sure. Really nice house, though." Autumn shakes her head, still not able to get past wanting to call Sherry's house her own. "Do you want to pay a visit to Malcolm's neighbor tonight?"

It doesn't take me long to reach a conclusion on that one. "Sherry said Rochelle Howey is in her twenties and looking for a husband. I'm highly doubting the likelihood of finding her at home on a Saturday night."

"I see your point. We can start there tomorrow."

"Thanks for helping me try to figure all this out, Autumn."

She reaches for my arm and squeezes it. "What are best friends for? Besides, I could get a home out of this."

I laugh. "You might want to run it by Aaron first to make sure he likes the house before you go making any offers."

She drops me off at home with a promise to pick me up in the morning so we can continue our sleuthing.

I walk into my empty house. It's a little depressing coming home to no one. Maybe I should get a cat. I heat up some leftovers for dinner and take a shower. I'm just getting settled on the couch to watch some TV when the doorbell rings.

"Who could that be?" I ask myself. Another side effect of living alone is talking to myself since there's no one else to talk to. I get up to answer the door, and as soon as I see who is standing on my doorstep, I instantly regret it. "Detective Lange, what are you doing here?"

"I came to find out what you were doing at Sherry Monaghan's house this evening."

Apparently, Autumn and I weren't as inconspicuous as we thought. Detective Lange saw us after all.

Chapter Eight

"Aren't you going to invite me in?" he asks when I don't respond.

"You've already searched the place. What more can you possibly want from me?"

"A confession would be nice."

I cross my arms in the doorway. "I'm not confessing to something I didn't do. Why don't you try finding the real guilty party instead of hounding me?"

"Would you like to come down to the station? Because the way I see it, I'm doing you yet another favor by coming here."

He certainly has a unique way of looking at things, and it's clear he believes he's telling the truth.

"I've already told you everything I know. I'm not withholding information, and I willingly let you search my house. I don't see how I can be any more cooperative."

"You can explain the wine bottle and why you went to see Sherry Monaghan."

"I already told you the wine was my grandmother's. I have nothing more to say on the matter. As for going to see Sherry, I thought an ex-wife might hold a grudge against her ex-husband." I debate telling him more and decide it actually helps my case to do so. "And I was surprised to find out Malcolm was previously married."

"He never told you?" Detective Lange asks.

"You've read the emails."

"Yes, but I'm sure you two also talked on the phone. Mentioning a divorce is more of a conversation to bring up on a phone call than in an email."

I agree with his logic there. "He never told me."

"Then how did you find out? Are you conducting your own investigation?" He cocks his head at me and narrows his eyes, like he's trying to see inside my mind.

"Wouldn't you if you were in my shoes? You keep accusing me of murder. Of course, I'm going to try to find the real guilty party so I can put an end to all of this. The only thing I've done wrong here is agree to a date with a man I thought I could trust."

"And now you think he wasn't such a good guy?"

I shrug. "I really don't know. He withheld information from me, but I guess I did the same to him."

"How so?" he pries.

"It's not really important. I didn't open up much about myself. Maybe he was doing the same until he felt I was trustworthy."

"So you went to ask Sherry about him," he says.

I nod. "Is that so wrong?"

"Did she accuse you of murdering Malcolm?"

"No." I'm not going to mention that Sherry admitted to still being in love with Malcolm. Not until I figure out what that actually means.

"I'm surprised. I thought she'd jump on the chance to accuse the woman her ex-husband was currently seeing."

There's only one reason why he'd say that. "You know," I say. "You figured out she's still in love with him."

"It was pretty obvious."

"Yet you don't suspect her of killing him?"

"Why would she?"

"I don't know. Maybe because he was going on a date with me." Seriously, is he so focused on me being the murderer that he can't see any other possibility?

"It doesn't add up."

"But *I* do? Me?" I point to my chest. "The woman who never even met him in person? What reason could I possibly have for wanting to kill him?" I hold up a hand to stop him from speaking. "And don't tell me it was to get his job. I said I want to teach before I retire. Not now."

"Here's what I think. I think you went to see if Sherry blamed you, too. Or maybe you'd heard that Sherry had a tendency to show up where Malcolm was, and you were afraid she was at the park last night and saw you kill him."

"That doesn't make sense. If she saw me kill him, she would have gone to the police."

"You're admitting you killed him," he says with a smug expression.

"No. I'm admitting your logic is severely flawed."

"Sydney, we both know you did this. I'm going to prove it. It's only a matter of when."

Can you file harassment charges against police detectives who are investigating you for murder? "We're finished here," I say, closing the door in his face.

It's probably not smart to make him angry with me, but clearly, being nice to him and cooperating with the investigation didn't work any better. I lock the door and turn off the front porch light. Is it wrong that I'm hoping Detective Lange trips down my stairs?

I opt to meet Autumn at the diner Sunday morning instead of having her pick me up. Mostly it's because I woke up early and couldn't sit still in my house alone waiting for her to arrive. I'm on my third cup of coffee when she joins me in the booth.

"Hey. Did you sleep at all? You look awful."

"Thanks. You're so sweet," I say.

"Sorry. Did you order yet?"

"I got you a western omelet."

"Thanks."

The waitress comes over to pour Autumn's coffee.

"So, Detective Lange paid me a visit last night."

"At home? What is wrong with that guy?"

Too many things to list. "He knows we were at Sherry's."

"Man, I thought we were pretty stealthy about it."

"He must know your license plate number."

"Figures. The man has too much time on his hands, probably because he's not looking into actual suspects on this case."

No argument from me there.

The waitress returns with our meals, and we dig right in.

"How are things with you and Aaron?" I ask.

"Okay. He's working today."

Since Aaron and Autumn opened the youth center together, they usually have their hands full seven days a week. Aaron is also a licensed contractor, and he takes on a lot of side jobs to help pay the bills.

"Did you tell him about Sherry's house?" I ask.

She bobs her head since her mouth is full. She raises her napkin in front of her face. "He knows which one it is. He really likes it. If only she'd put it on the market. I think it would be perfect for us."

"Well, then I hope she decides to sell, too." We finish eating our food, and I flag down the waitress for the check. She pulls it from her apron pocket and places it on the table before clearing our plates.

Autumn's phone vibrates on the table three times in quick succession. She snatches it up and reads the screen.

"I can't believe this," she says. "There's an emergency at the youth center. I have to go right now."

"Is everything okay?"

"I don't know. Something about a broken pipe. Hopefully, Aaron can fix it before we get too much water damage." She looks down at the check.

"I'll take care of the bill. Just go. Good luck."

"Thanks, Syd." She grabs her purse and rushes out of the diner.

I get my wallet and pull out enough cash for the bill and a nice tip. I place the money on top of the check and stand up. As I'm walking to the exit, I run into Nolan Lange, Detective Lange's younger brother who moved away about three years ago.

"Sydney Warner?" he asks me.

I nod. "Hi, Nolan. I thought you fled Swan Creek for good."

One side of his mouth curves up. "I thought so, too, but I just moved back to town. I got transferred for work."

If I remember correctly, Nolan is a reporter. "Well, welcome back. You aren't staying with your brother, are you?"

I can't help asking on the off chance that Drew sent Nolan to spy on me.

"Heck no!" He answers so quickly it makes me laugh.

"Do I detect some bad blood between brothers with that reaction?" I ask.

"That's right. You're a psychologist." He snaps his fingers. "I bet you read a lot into that response, huh?"

"I try not to analyze people twenty-four seven, but it's hard to turn off my internal people reader sometimes."

"Don't get me wrong. I love my brother, but he can be a little over-the-top at times. He means well, though."

"I think he means to put me in handcuffs," I say. "I'm sure you've heard about the murder Friday night." Being in the news business, he has to be up to speed, even if he did just get back in town.

Nolan offers me a small smile. "For what it's worth, I don't think you're capable of murder. I mean, you probably would have killed my brother by now if you were, right?"

I laugh. "Yeah, probably. He has it in for me."

"Drew is mad at the world. Don't take it personally. He doesn't even like *me* that much." He bobs one shoulder. "I guess it couldn't have been easy when our parents announced they were having a baby when Drew was ten. He loved being an only child, and then I came along and ruined everything for him."

"Does he really see it that way? That's awful."

"It's okay. I can't blame him, but it's not like I asked my parents to have me either."

"Of course not. I don't see how he can fault you for it."

"Drew has this need to assign blame."

"Believe me; I've noticed."

Nolan smirks. "Yeah, I guess you have. But he's not always the best at assigning it to the right person."

"That's scary considering his line of work."

"Tell me about it. When he told my parents and me that he wanted to be a police detective, I thought it was a terrible idea. He jumps to conclusions and tries to stick to them no matter how wrong they might turn out to be. I think he hates to admit when he makes a mistake."

"Why do I suddenly have no faith in the SCPD?" I ask.

"Sorry, this must sound awful, and I'm sure you don't want to talk about Drew." He motions to the door. "You were on your way out, weren't you?"

I nod.

"Can I walk you to your car?"

"Sure, but you really don't have to."

"I insist." He opens the door for me.

I step outside, noticing how mild the temperature is today. Maybe we're in for an early spring. That would be nice.

"So, big plans for this beautiful Sunday?" he asks, following me to my car.

I don't know Nolan well. He always seemed like a nice guy. He was on the football team and in the National Honor Society, but it's not like we were friends. And he is Drew Lange's brother.

He stops walking and faces me. "What is it, Sydney?"

"Nothing. No plans."

"Really? I'd think you'd be trying to figure out who killed Malcolm Monaghan. That's what I'd be doing if I were in your shoes."

"You would?"

"Do you know how many times Drew accused me of things when we were growing up? I felt like I was always on trial. I know what it's like to be on the receiving end of his accusations. Let me help."

"No, that's really not necessary."

"I know it's not necessary, but I just moved back here, and I could use a friend. And something to do on a Sunday. My job doesn't officially start for a few more days, and I live in a tiny apartment by myself. I have nothing better to do. You'd be saving me from a day of watching Netflix."

He is a reporter, so he's probably skilled in interviewing people. He could be helpful to have with me when I go talk to Malcom's neighbor, Rochelle Howey. "Only if you're sure," I say.

He smiles and nods. "Leave your car here. If my brother is following you, it might trick him into thinking you're still at the diner. I'll drive us." He grabs his keys from his pocket.

"Wait. Weren't you going to the diner for breakfast? You didn't even get to eat anything."

His face turns red. "Okay, don't judge me, but I sort of ate before I left my apartment this morning. I was only going to the diner for some human interaction."

He's lonely. Aw. "No judgement," I say. "But I do have a question. Why are you doing this? We barely know each other, and you're going to come with me to question a suspect in a murder."

"Apologizing for my brother's behavior has sort of become second nature to me. I guess I want people to know not all Lange men are bad guys." He looks down. "Not that Drew is a bad guy. He just tends to see the worst in people." He points to the white mustang. "This is my car."

"You drive a mustang?" I ask.

"Yeah, why? Does that mean something?"

I laugh. "I'm not psychoanalyzing you. Relax. The mustang has always been one of my favorite cars." I don't tell him I'm not a fan of white cars.

"Oh. Well, hop in." He unlocks the doors, and we both get in.

"Where are we headed?" he asks after starting the engine.

"Oh." I pull up Malcolm's address, since Rochelle lives next door. "Do you know where Apple Orchard Road is?" I ask.

"I think I remember." He pulls out of the parking lot. "I always thought it was odd that there's no apple orchard on that road."

"I know. There is a farm, though. I think it was originally called Apple Orchard Farm, but it changed hands."

"Hmm. I never knew that." There's a moment of awkward silence before he says, "So, I know you found the body on Friday. What were you doing there?"

I look down at my hands, which are laced in my lap. "I was on a date with Malcolm. Or I was meeting him there for one. I guess the date didn't happen since he was already dead when I arrived."

"I'm so sorry. Had you known him long?"

"Not at all. We'd only talked for about a month."

"Why does Drew think you killed him then?"

"Convenience, I suppose. I found the body and was supposed to meet Malcolm there. And then your brother found a bottle of wine in my grandmother's wine cellar that matched the bottle Malcolm was poisoned with."

"I see. No wonder he's determined to prove you're guilty."

Does that mean Nolan thinks I'm guilty after hearing that, too? I cock my head at him. "Did you change your mind about my innocence?"

"No, sorry. That's not what I mean. You see, when Drew finds even a shred of evidence, or what might be evidence, he runs with it. You said it was your grandmother's wine cellar?"

"Yeah, but she's no longer alive. I live in her house."

"Oh, and if you ask Drew, that bottle now belongs to you, making you the guilty party."

"I guess it was really stupid of me to tell him he could search my home."

"If you ask me, it was smart. Any other cop would have realized you'd have to be innocent to allow that." He dips his head to the side. "Drew, on the other hand, probably thought you were being cocky and thinking he'd never solve the case."

"Great. So I basically made this into more of a challenge for him."

"Unfortunately, yes. He probably saw it as you throwing down the gauntlet."

"You couldn't have come back to town a few days sooner and explained your brother to me before I went and made a mess of my situation?" I tease.

"Sorry. If I'd known, I would have." He turns to look at me. "You really don't remember me, do you?"

"Of course, I remember you. We just didn't know each other well at all."

"Other than having classes together or when I delivered the Valentine chocolate roses every year for National Honor Society."

"I still don't know who sent those." I always assumed it was Autumn, but she denied it. They stopped my senior year. It was the only year I didn't get one. Wait. I turn to Nolan, who meets my gaze. "Was it—?"

"Me," he says.

Chapter Nine

I can't believe this. I never knew, nor would I have ever guessed Nolan Lange was my secret Valentine admirer. "But why?"

"Your freshman year, we had study hall together. You sat in front of me. I used to ask to borrow a pen from you just about every day to try to get you to talk to me."

And I would hand him a pen without saying a word. I put my hand to my mouth. "You must have thought I was so rude."

He laughs. "No, I thought you were really into your schoolwork."

I used to spend study hall reading. Not for class, though. I went through a period where I read all the classics for fun. "I'm so sorry. I feel awful."

"Don't. I should have talked to you instead of finding dumb ways to try to get your attention. Your sophomore year was really embarrassing."

"What do you mean?" I don't remember anything embarrassing happening that year.

"I wished you a happy birthday during the morning announcements."

"I figured Autumn put you up to that. She always loved embarrassing me on my birthday. She'd insist on taking me out after school, and she'd tell our waiter or waitress it was my birthday so they'd get all the other waitstaff to come over and sing to me."

"Oh, wow. You didn't know, and I just told you." He shakes his head. "Now I'm embarrassed all over again."

"Don't be. That was nice of you to do."

"Nothing tops my senior year, though."

"Now you have to tell me because I can't think of what you did that year either."

"The homecoming game. All the players gave their jerseys to girls to wear on game day."

The football jersey that somehow wound up in my locker. "I thought one of the players put it in my locker as a joke." I never went to a single game, so I had no idea what Nolan's number was to identify the jersey that way, and our school was too cheap to put the players' names on the backs of the jerseys.

He laughs. "I can't believe I spent years being embarrassed about all those things, and you never had a clue."

I couldn't pick up on clues like those, and I'm supposed to catch a killer? I'm not liking my chances at all anymore. "I feel so stupid."

"Don't. It's all on me. I was too shy to talk to you." He pulls onto Apple Orchard Road. "Which house is it?"

"Um." I peer out the window. "Malcolm is number one hundred and twenty-four, so Rochelle is either one hundred and twenty-two or one hundred and twenty-six."

"Well, one twenty-two looks empty, like no one lives there, so I'm going to guess it's one twenty-six."

"Good assumption," I say.

He pulls into the driveway and parks.

"You can wait here if you'd like. I don't want Drew getting upset with you for questioning this woman." And I feel bad enough after hearing how oblivious I was to him in high school.

"And let you question a potential murderer on your own?" He shakes his head. "No way." He undoes his seat belt and gets out of the car.

I follow him to the front door. Hopefully, Rochelle wasn't out too late last night looking for her future husband, or she may not be up yet. I ring the doorbell.

It takes a few minutes, but finally, the door opens. Rochelle is a pretty woman with curly blonde hair. She's dressed in leggings, a fitted tank top, and a crop crewneck sweatshirt. "Can I help you?"

"Are you Rochelle Howey?" I ask.

"Yeah. If you're selling something, I'm not interested."

"No, we're not. We're actually here because of your neighbor."

Rochelle swipes a curl from her face. "Malcolm. It's a shame what happened to him."

"Then you heard."

"Yeah, I heard. This is why you shouldn't meet total strangers from a dating app. Everybody always thinks these things only happen to women, but if you've seen Malcolm, you know how attractive that man was."

Great, she thinks Malcolm's date killed him. "Did he talk to you about his date?" I ask, glad I didn't offer my name in case he told her that, too.

"A little. Not much. I saw him when he was heading out." She narrows her eyes at us. "Are you two cops or reporters or something?"

"I'm a reporter," Nolan says. "Anything you can remember from Friday night would be very helpful to the piece I'm working on."

"Oh. Okay. Well, I saw Malcolm leave his house. He was dressed nicely, and since it was Valentine's Day, I was curious where he was going. He didn't have a girlfriend." She rolls her eyes. "He did have an ex-wife, though. Crazy woman. She'd show up at his house unannounced."

Seems like Sherry made it a habit to show up wherever Malcolm was. And the fact that she didn't question me makes me wonder if she's guilty after all. However, Rochelle is admitting to watching Malcolm as well, whether she realizes it or not. She had to be watching him to see him leave home Friday night.

Nolan's been asking Rochelle questions, but I've been lost in my own train of thought. I focus on the conversation again.

"Did you ever see Malcolm and Sherry fight?"

"All the time. She was trying to get back together with him. She'd apologize for messing around behind his back. Said she did it because she wanted to feel loved again, or something like that. Then he'd tell her it's over, and he'd either shut the door in her face or he'd take off in his car." She flips her hair over her shoulder. "I told him he should tell her he and I were together to get her to back off."

"Were you two dating?" Nolan asks her.

She twirls a lock of hair. "Well, I don't know if you'd call it that. We flirted a lot. He was definitely interested, but you have to be careful these days. I didn't want to rush into anything."

"Of course," Nolan says, but the look he gives me when Rochelle gazes next door at Malcolm's house tells me he's not buying her story at all. Neither am I.

"Do you have any idea who might have wanted Malcolm dead?" I ask her.

Rochelle looks at me again and lets out a deep sigh. I can smell the remnants of alcohol on her breath. She must have had a late night partying. "Well, there was this student that came by his house twice."

"A student?" Nolan asks. He's not aware that Malcolm was a psychology professor.

"Yeah, I think he was yelling about a grade he got on a paper. He threatened Malcolm. Said he wasn't going to let a middle-aged man ruin his scholarship over one paper." Rochelle scoffs. "Can you believe that? Malcolm wasn't middle-aged."

"Do you know who the student was?" Nolan asks her.

She shakes her head. "No, but he was here twice. I guess Malcolm didn't change his grade. The guy was really angry. He threw a rock at Malcolm's front window. He missed, which is ironic because I think he's a baseball player. If you look at the siding on Malcolm's house, you'll see the crack where the rock hit it."

"Thank you, Rochelle. You've been very helpful," Nolan tells her.

"Do you want to get a picture of me for your article?" She tilts her head and poses.

"Sorry, but I didn't get enough room for accompanying photos with the article. If my editor changes his mind about that, I'll be sure to contact you." He smiles and dips his head at her before turning back toward his car.

"You handled that like a pro. I'd even say better than your brother would have," I tell him as we get into the Mustang.

"Don't let him hear you say that. He'd really come gunning for you." Nolan pulls into Malcom's driveway next door.

"Rochelle is right. I can see the broken siding below the front window."

"She must be wrong about the kid playing baseball, though, right? I mean, if he was playing on a scholarship, he wouldn't miss a target that large."

"Unless he missed on purpose. Maybe he only wanted to intimidate Malcolm but not get charges pressed against him for destruction of property."

"He still ruined the siding. Malcolm could have pressed charges."

"You want to look into this student next?"

"You really don't have to help me. I've taken up enough of your Sunday as it is."

He turns to face me. "Are you kidding me? All my life, I've tried to one-up my brother. You're giving me a chance to show him he's not the smartest Lange brother after all."

"Why do I get the feeling you've proven that before, Mr. National Honor Society?"

He laughs. "I guess Drew and I don't have the best relationship."

I'm sure the age difference doesn't help, but then again, I'd think that would cut down on the competition that might exist between siblings since they weren't in school at the same time growing up. Now it probably doesn't matter much, though. Age gaps sort of disappear once both people are adults.

"How do we find out who this student is?" I ask, wanting to change the subject because it's clearly making Nolan uncomfortable judging by the way he's gripping the steering wheel even though the car is parked.

"Talk to one of Malcolm's colleagues?"

"The only one I've spoken to was gunning for Malcolm's courses."

"Ah, so he might not be much help."

"I don't know. I guess it couldn't hurt to go see him again. He lives in town."

Nolan starts the car. "Tell me where to go."

It's odd how easy he is to talk to considering we didn't talk much at all the entire time we grew up together. "You said your job is what brought you back to Swan Creek," I say after giving him the directions to Gerard Cowen's house.

"Yeah. I was working at a small paper in Chicago. I hated how cold it was there. After growing up here with the mild winters, it was like a shock to my system. And being the new guy made me low man on the totem pole. I was sent out in the field all the time. I couldn't take it anymore. So when a position opened up here, I applied for it."

"Good for you. I mean, if you wanted to come back home, that is."

"I did. My parents are gone now."

"I'm so sorry."

"No, I mean they moved to Florida. That's where they retired about five years ago."

"Oh, mine too."

"Something else we have in common," he says.

"What was the first thing we had in common?" I turn to face him.

"Plenty actually. We both live here. We're both single. We're investigating the same case. The list goes on and on."

I laugh. "Were you this funny in high school?"

"No. I was socially awkward. If not for being good at football, I'm not sure I would have had many friends."

"I have a hard time believing that."

"It's true. It was tough growing up in Drew's shadow. The teachers remembered him and assumed I'd be just like him.

We're really nothing alike, though."

"I'm noticing that." I smile at him.

"I was able to change their minds about me, but it's hard to ignore all the eye rolls and mumbling on the first day of class."

"Okay, but none of the kids we went to school with knew Drew. He was already gone before any of us were in school."

"True, he was a sophomore when I was in kindergarten. But Drew had this group he hung out with. They were always together. Until I found football and made friends with the guys on the team, I didn't really have friends. I was chubby and had a speech impediment in elementary school. I got picked on a lot."

"Aw, kids can be cruel."

"Is this the house we're looking for?" he asks.

"Yup, this is the one. He has a little, yappy dog, by the way. I hope you're not allergic, although it might be some sort of poodle mix, so there's a chance it doesn't shed."

Nolan cuts the engine. "I'm not allergic anyway."

"I'm not sure Gerard will be too happy to see me again."

"I can do most of the talking. I'll play up the reporter angle like I did with Rochelle."

"You're pretty handy to have around," I say.

He smiles and turns away as if embarrassed.

I ring the doorbell.

Like I thought, Gerard isn't exactly happy I've returned. "You again. What is it this time?"

"Mr. Cowen, I'm Nolan Lange. I'm doing a story on Malcolm Monaghan, and I was hoping you'd be able to answer a few questions for me. Sydney here told me you were very helpful when she spoke to you previously."

Gerard eyes me suspiciously. "Did you check out the ex-wife?"

"You were right about her," I say, figuring that might help this get off on the right foot.

He bobs his head. "What else do you want to know?" His dog comes to the door and stretches like it just woke up. Gerard shoos it back into the house.

"We heard Malcolm Monaghan was having trouble with one of his students," Nolan starts. "Apparently, the student failed a paper and was worried about losing his scholarship because of it."

Gerard huffs. "I'm taking over Malcolm's classes, but I haven't met with the students yet, obviously. I can access grades to see who is failing, though. Come in." He turns and walks inside.

I close the door behind me so the dog doesn't run out. I bend down and read the name on the collar. "Mitzy. Hi, Mitzy." The dog licks my nose. I pet his head before following Gerard and Nolan into the living room.

Gerard gets on his iPad again. "Let's see. There are five courses. Any idea which one this kid was in?"

"No, sorry. Malcolm's neighbor thought he was a baseball player, though."

Gerard furrows his brow. "I might know who that is. Hang on." He swipes the screen a few times. "Okay, Emmett Michaelson. He's in the only entry level course Malcolm teaches. I figured a baseball player would be taking psychology for general education credits."

"Why? Because athletes can't possibly be smart?" Nolan asks him, clearly taking offense to Gerard's comment.

Gerard lowers the iPad, and I'm afraid he's not going to help us. "No, because the athletes are locked into classes at particular times of the day due to their sports schedules. The only class Malcolm teaches that fits that time would be his gen ed psychology requirement."

"Sorry," Nolan says. "I was an athlete. I'm used to certain stereotypes."

"I understand." Gerard raises the iPad again. "Anyway, Emmett Michaelson failed his last paper. His overall grade for the class was already in danger before that, so this must have been the assignment that pushed him toward failing for the semester."

"But it's still early in the semester, isn't it?"

"It is, but looking at the syllabus, this paper counted for forty percent of the final average."

Ouch. "Is that typical for so early in the semester?"

"No. Malcolm didn't assign many papers, though. It appears the one at the end of the semester is worth forty percent of the grade as well, with smaller assignments in between making up the rest. I can see how this kid might panic over his grade."

"But you don't know him personally, correct?" Nolan asks.

"No, I do not. I suppose I will get to know him, though."

"Could you do me a favor?" I ask. "If this Emmett Michaelson does anything suspicious, will you let me know?" I reach into my coat pocket, hoping I have a gas station receipt or something on me to write down my number.

"Suspicious? You think he had something to do with Malcolm's murder?"

"Depends how big his scholarship is and how much Emmett needs it," I say, giving up on my search. "I'd be happy to give you my number."

"Or I could give you mine," Nolan says.

"No offense to either of you, but if I suspect this kid of killing someone, even someone I didn't care for, I'll call the police." He closes the door in our faces.

Chapter Ten

Nolan drives us back to the diner where my car is parked. Since he's been nice enough to help me all morning, I insist on buying him lunch as a thank you.

"This really isn't necessary," Nolan says.

"Neither was you spending your day helping me."

The door to the diner opens, and Detective Lange comes walking in.

"Oh no." My gaze locks on him, but he hasn't noticed me yet.

"What is it?" Nolan turns around in his seat. "Oh." He faces me again. "This probably isn't going to go well. Let me apologize in advance."

"You don't have to apologize for his behavior," I say as Detective Lange spots us. "He sees us and is heading this way." I sip my unsweetened iced tea with lemon.

Nolan eats a French fry, feigning nonchalance.

"Well, what do we have here? My little brother and the woman I suspect of murder. That's an interesting combination," Detective Lange says.

I don't believe it's a coincidence that brought him here. "Did you sit in the parking lot watching my car all day?" I ask him.

He scoffs. "I had one of the rookies do that for me. He called when you two arrived. Imagine my surprise when I found out you'd spent the morning with my brother."

"You spotted my car, came in to find me, didn't, and then got someone else to stake out the parking lot for you until I came back. Tell me; do you do any police work on your own? I mean you admitted it was another officer who got into Malcolm's phone, and now this."

"I found the bottle of wine in your house all by myself, now didn't I?"

I'm not going to give him credit for anything in this investigation. "Actually, I gave you permission to search my house and the wine cellar, so you did have help there. Mine. And you jumped to the wrong conclusion about that wine, so I'm definitely not giving you any points for that one."

Nolan smiles and quickly covers it up by pretending to wipe his mouth with his napkin. "What do you want, Drew?"

"To know what you're doing with my murder suspect."

"Sydney and I are catching up. We are old classmates, you know." He picks up a French fry. "Fry? Or is Annabelle complaining about your weight again?"

Detective Lange's composure falters for a split second, but he recovers and says, "I'd ask about your significant other, but since there isn't one to speak of..." His smug look is the only conclusion to his thought.

"Yes, well we always did have different goals in life, didn't we?" Nolan asks.

"Yeah, I'm out there helping people every day, and you're..." Detective Lange rubs the scruff on his chin. "What are you up to these days, little brother? Besides running home after failing in a big city?"

"He didn't fail in the city. He didn't like living there. And what's your excuse? You never left this town." Not that I did either, so my argument is really weak.

"Why would I leave? I want to protect and serve the town that raised me."

The town that raised him? This guy thinks he's way more important than he is. Most of the people who lived here when he was growing up have left by now, retiring elsewhere. And those that stayed probably wouldn't remember Drew's name or face.

"Sure, Drew. You're a real town hero. I suppose you've found the person who really murdered Malcolm Monaghan then."

Detective Lange raises his hand to gesture to me. "You're eating with her."

"No, I'm eating with Sydney."

Detective Lange bends down and lowers his voice. "Nolan, you're my little brother, so let me give you some brotherly advice. Run as far away from this one as you can get. She's trouble, and if you let her, she will bring you down with her."

"Thanks for the advice, Brother." He stresses the last word, and it makes me question if he's ever called Drew that before in their lives. I'd bet my life savings he hasn't. "Let me return the favor. If you pursue this path you're on and try to blame Sydney, you're going to make a laughing stock out of yourself in the end. The real killer is getting away and laughing at you in the process. I know you like getting fan mail and all, but getting it from felons you failed to convict isn't the way I'd go if I were you. I'm just saying." He sips his ginger ale.

Detective Lange stands up tall, adjusts his jacket, and walks away.

"Nicely handled," I say. I give Nolan credit for keeping his composure, but I can also tell how much it bothers him that he and Drew fight like this. I'm getting the feeling Nolan only ever wanted a protective big brother who loved him. Instead, he got Drew. A brother who resented Nolan for even being born.

"I probably ruined his life by moving back here."

"It's hard for me to feel sorry for him when he's trying to ruin my life."

"Yeah, I think you've mentioned that once before. Don't worry, Syd. I'm not looking for sympathy." Hearing him call me Syd like we've been friends forever is oddly comforting.

"Why are you so easy to talk to?" I ask him.

"I'm really not. I just look good in comparison to a certain other Lange brother."

"Please don't tell me there's another." Drew does exhibit signs of classic middle child syndrome. "A brother ten years Drew's senior, maybe."

Nolan laughs. "No, it's only the two of us. That's all you get."

"It's plenty," I say before realizing he might think I'm insulting him as well as Drew. "I just mean we don't need another Drew. You're fine."

"One day, you're going to have to give me your professional analysis of my brother."

I whistle. "That would be a doozy. I'm not sure I want to dive into his psyche."

"I don't blame you."

"What was it like growing up with him? Did he always run to your parents to complain about you?"

"No, it was more that he ignored me. I think he tried to pretend I didn't exist. My parents worked a lot, so they didn't really notice."

Poor Nolan. I know he said he's not looking for sympathy, but I can't help feeling sorry for all he's been through, and it makes me feel worse about not giving him the time of day in high school. How could I have been so oblivious at the time?

"Tell me about your job. It's got to be emotionally taxing listening to people's problems all the time."

"Yeah, but when someone has a breakthrough…" I smile. "I can't explain the happiness I feel for them."

"And knowing you helped them get there."

I lean toward him across the table. "Want to know a secret?"

He nods and leans forward to mimic my stance.

"Most people already know the answers they're looking for in life. They just need to hear themselves voice them out loud and have someone listen."

"Does that mean you're really doodling in your notebook during your sessions with patients?" One side of his mouth curves up.

"Not just doodling. Sometimes, I write poetry." I laugh to let him know I'm only kidding.

"You almost had me for a minute there. I was about to ask if you've had any published."

"Not since junior high when we had that literary magazine at school."

"I remember that. We'd get to submit drawings, poetry, and short stories."

I nod. "I had exactly one poem accepted. I think it was about the sunrise or something like that. It was an assignment for my English class, and Mrs. Sabino told me I should submit it."

"And a published author was born," he says, raising his glass to me.

I press a finger to my lips. "Shh. Keep it down. I try not to be recognized in public."

He laughs. "I really wish I'd had the courage to talk to you in high school. I think we would've been…" He pauses, a dead giveaway that he's not going to say what he really wanted to. "Close."

The waitress comes over with our check, but before she places it on the table, she says, "Is there anything else I can get you?"

Nolan looks to me.

"No, I think we're all set," I say.

"Okay, then I'll leave this here for whenever you're ready." She places the check on the table, and Nolan snatches it up.

"Uh-uh," I say. "We agreed this is on me."

"Technically, I never agreed. You just said you were buying me lunch."

"Exactly. This is lunch."

"But this one is on me." He removes his wallet and pulls out several bills, which he hands to the waitress. "Keep the change."

"Thank you. Enjoy your day," she says before walking away.

"Nolan." I level him with a look.

"Okay, fine. I don't want you to think I'm not a man of my word, even if I didn't agree to letting you pay to begin with. So here's what we'll do. We'll meet for lunch tomorrow, and you can pay then."

I clamp my jaw shut so my surprise doesn't show to everyone in the diner. He's asking me out. And in a pretty adorable way. I extend my hand to him. "Shake on it?"

He smiles and shakes my hand. "It's a date," he says as if he's not sure I picked up on that already.

"I have patients in the morning until noon," I tell him.

"Want to meet here at noon then?"

"Sounds like a plan." I stand up. "Thank you for lunch and this morning."

"Hey, if I can be of any more help, say the word. I have nothing to do for the next few days until my job starts. And something tells me Drew and Annabelle won't be inviting me over any time soon."

"No, I wouldn't hold your breath waiting for that invite."

We get out of the booth, and he walks me to my car. I can tell he doesn't want to part ways yet, but he's not going to push to spend the afternoon together, too. After all, this is the first time we've actually said more than a sentence to each other. So why is it so easy to talk to him?

"See you tomorrow?" he says.

"Tomorrow." I open my car door and get in. Since I'm not sure where to go next with this investigation, I decide to drive to the youth center and see if Autumn needs help. Not that I'm a plumber. I'm talking about emotional support. She might need to vent about how much it will cost to fix or how long they're going to need to close for repairs. I want to make sure I'm there for her.

I pull up and see a plumber's van leaving the parking lot. I get out of my car and walk right up to the front door, which is unlocked. Aaron is inside, wearing his tool belt and looking like he went twelve rounds in the ring with an octopus. He's soaking wet from head to toe.

"You okay there, Aaron?" I ask.

He looks up at me and shakes water from his hair. "It's a look, right?"

"It suits you. You're like Aquaman."

"Just what I've always wanted. Did Autumn call you?"

"No. I was with her this morning when she found out about the pipe." I jerk a thumb over my shoulder. I saw the plumber leave. Is it fixed?"

"Yeah, now we have to deal with the cleanup. I don't suppose you're good at mopping up massive amounts of water," he says.

"Direct me to a mop," I say.

It's dark by the time we get the youth center mostly dried up. There are giant fans on the floor, trying to air them out. We all look like we ran marathons, and my arms are killing me from pushing the mop across the floor over and over again.

"Thank you for coming," Autumn says, handing me a bottle of water.

I take a big gulp and then laugh, nearly choking.

"What?" she asks.

"We spent hours trying to get rid of all the water in this place, and here we are gulping it down." I hold up the bottle.

"How did the interrogation go? Was Malcolm's neighbor home?"

"Yeah, Nolan and I talked to her."

"Nolan?" She narrows her eyes at me. "Why do I feel like I missed a key piece to your day?"

"Because you did. I forgot he showed up after you left the diner." I fill her in on everything that happened, and she swats my arm several times. "Ow!"

"Sorry, but I can't believe you didn't tell me this hours ago. You had a date."

"It was not a date."

"He bought you lunch."

"I bought you breakfast this morning. I'm pretty sure we aren't dating. I don't think Aaron would allow it."

"Stop deflecting."

"Stop using my own psychology terms against me."

"You like him," she says. "I can tell."

I don't lie to Autumn. Ever. So I can't tell her she's wrong. "It's weird, right? I mean, we weren't friends growing up, and the guy I was supposedly seeing died two days ago. I shouldn't be getting involved with someone new."

"Okay, first, you and Malcolm exchanged emails and talked on the phone twice. It's not like you were really dating or like you were exclusive. Second, Nolan was really cute in high school. What does he look like now? And when are you seeing him again?"

"He's still really cute, and we're having lunch together tomorrow."

She shrieks. "I love this!"

"Yeah, except for the part where he's Drew Lange's brother."

"Ugh, yeah, I forgot about that part. Can you imagine if Drew becomes your brother-in-law one day?"

I hold up both hands. "Let's not get ahead of ourselves."

"Speaking of Drew, what are you going to do about him? He doesn't seem to be pursuing any other suspects in this case."

"I know." I have to find out who killed Malcolm. And I need to do it fast, or Nolan and I will be having any future dates in the visitation room at the county jail.

Chapter Eleven

I look at the clock for the third time in the past ten minutes. I know I should be paying better attention to Bailey Sinclair, the patient I'm currently in a session with, but I'm nervous for my date with Nolan. The fact that my last date ended with me in a police interrogation room has me a little on edge.

"What do you think?" Bailey asks me. "Am I overreacting?"

I clear my throat. "What I think doesn't really matter. Do *you* think you're overreacting?"

"I didn't think so. I mean, he sent her a card for Valentine's Day. Who sends their ex-girlfriend a Valentine when he has a new girlfriend?"

That does sound bad. I need to start paying attention to her. "Bailey, your feelings are completely justified. You want to know if he's as committed to your relationship as you are, and it's hard to commit fully to someone when you're still hung up on the past."

"Yes! See, you get it. Why doesn't he? When I tried to tell him how I feel, he said I was being jealous and overly clingy."

"What reason did he have for sending her the Valentine?"

"He said he doesn't think you stop caring for people even if you stop loving them."

I nod and jot some notes into my notebook. "That's valid. You can wish an ex well in life, but I think the approach you should take is that some people might read into a Valentine as more than just well wishes or showing you still care about someone as a person. I'm sure he doesn't want to lead her on, right?"

"You mean in order for him to accept my feelings, I have to show I understand his but that I disagree with how he's showing them?"

"Yes. Checking in with someone shows you care. A Valentine is more for a romantic gesture. If you try explaining it to him that way, he might understand where you're coming from."

"Thanks, Dr. Warner. That makes a lot of sense. But how do I get over the fact that I don't really want him talking to his ex?"

"I think you need to ask yourself if you trust him or not. If you don't, then there's a bigger conversation you need to have with him."

The clock on the wall chimes. "I'm afraid that's all we have time for today."

Bailey stands up. "I hope when I come see you next week, I'll be telling you all about how much better my relationship with Elliot is."

I hope so, too, because the alternative is her crying on my couch and telling me about their breakup. She's young, only twenty-four, so the odds that Elliot is the one for her are pretty much up in the air still.

"Can I ask you a question?"

"Sure," I close the notebook and walk over to my desk to return it to the top drawer.

"Would you trust your boyfriend if he was still talking to his ex?"

It's hard to answer when I don't have a boyfriend. "Bailey, I don't think that's a general question with a concrete answer. I think it's specific to the person. You need to look at who Elliot is and determine if he's the type to stray from your relationship."

"I was afraid you'd say that," she says.

Most of the time, my patients know what I'm going to say before I say it. It's good because it means they have a good grasp on the situations they're dealing with. "Tell you what. I promise you that no matter what happens, you will get through it because you are a strong woman. You come here week after week and work through the things that are bothering you. That takes a lot of willpower. If Elliot doesn't appreciate you and treat you the way you deserve to be treated —"

"I'll find someone who does," she finishes for me with a smile. "Thanks, Dr. Warner. I feel better already."

I smile at her as she walks out. Then I grab my purse.

Lena pokes her head into the office. "Your one o'clock has to cancel. He had a death in his family, and he has to travel for the funeral services."

"Oh, poor Randy. I'll need to mail him a card."

"I'm running to the store on my lunch break. I can pick one up for you if you'd like."

"Thanks, Lena. Since he canceled, take an extra-long lunch. There's no need to come back before two."

"Sounds good. Thanks." She smiles and walks out.

I grab my keys and head to the diner.

Nolan is already there when I arrive. "Hey." He stands up to greet me, which is nice and very gentlemanly of him. I feel like I'm so far removed from the dating game I don't remember how to do this. Yet, somehow, I've had multiple dates in the past four days with two different men. I'm still not sure how I feel about that.

"Am I late?" I ask, slipping into the booth seat across from him.

"Not at all. I got here early." He places his napkin on his lap. "I told you my schedule is wide open at the moment." He holds up a finger. "And because of that, I emailed Gerard Cowen this morning and gave him my number. I realized we asked him to call us if anything happened with Emmett Michaelson, yet neither of us gave him our numbers."

"Good thinking."

The waitress comes to the table with a pot of coffee in her hand, and I flip the mug in front of me over so she can pour me a cup. "Are you two ready to order?"

Nolan motions to me. I haven't given much thought to what I want to eat. I actually skipped breakfast this morning, though, so I'm pretty hungry.

"I'd love some strawberry crepes," I say.

She nods to me. "And for you, sir?"

"I'll take a cheeseburger deluxe and another iced tea."

"I'll put your order in right away." She dashes off.

"How long have you been here if you're already on your second iced tea?" I ask him.

"Well, I got tired of staring at the same four walls at my apartment, so I got here about an hour ago. I drank a pot of coffee at home before this."

"Uh-oh, someone is severely over caffeinated. Maybe you should switch to water." I sip my coffee, which clearly has been sitting in the pot for a while. I shouldn't be surprised by that since it's lunchtime.

"You might be right, but I already ordered, and I hate to waste." He winks at me. "What's the rest of your day look like?"

"My one o'clock canceled on me. He had a death in the family. I have a two o'clock scheduled, and then I'm free. Mondays are usually my slow days."

"Do you ever do phone sessions?"

"Yes, I have two patients who are pretty much recluses. I do all of their sessions over the phone."

"Do you find that harder, not being able to read their body language and all?" he asks, seeming genuinely interested.

"At first it was, but I've been working with them both for so long now I've learned how to tell when they're holding back or not being totally truthful."

"Have you noticed common issues among your patients?"

"Money's a big one. Love. Acceptance. Really, most people want the same things in life."

He smiles at me. "I feel like I should schedule an appointment with you. I have a feeling you're really good at what you do."

"Thanks. I hope my patients think so."

The waitress returns with our meals. I'm always surprised by how quickly the kitchen puts out food here. "Let me know if you need anything else."

"Actually, I have a question, if you don't mind," I say.

"Sure." She smiles at me.

"You didn't happen to know Malcolm Monaghan, the man who was murdered at the park last Friday night, did you?"

"I saw that on the news. I recognized his picture on TV because he used to come here, but I never knew him by name."

"Do you know who he used to come in here with?" Nolan asks her.

"A woman. She had brown hair and brown eyes. She was pretty and the same age as him."

Sherry? "How long ago was that?" I ask.

"I think the last time I saw him was just a few weeks ago."

"And he was with that woman?" I ask.

She nods. "Yeah. They sat in the corner booth over there. That's where they usually sat."

"Usually? Are you saying they met here a lot?" How can this be? Malcolm was talking to me but still meeting his ex-wife?

"Yeah, usually once a week."

"Thank you," Nolan tells her.

She nods and walks away.

"Sydney, are you okay?" he asks me.

"Yeah, I guess. I just can't believe he was still seeing his ex-wife."

"His ex-wife who cheated on him and is currently living in their old house with her current boyfriend. The entire situation is pretty screwed-up if you ask me." He takes a big bite of his cheeseburger, and grease dribbles out onto the plate.

"I really thought he was a nice guy."

"I'm sorry. Maybe it's not what we're thinking, though. Maybe they were meeting to discuss the divorce."

"The divorce that happened a year ago? Not likely." It's clear from my meeting with Sherry that she's still in love with Malcolm. "I think Sherry was trying to win him back."

"It didn't work, though. He was planning to spend Valentine's Day with you."

Which could have sent Sherry over the edge. I could be dealing with a classic case of "If I can't have him, no one can" syndrome.

"You're thinking the same thing I am, aren't you?" Nolan asks.

"That Sherry killed Malcolm when her plan to win him back failed."

He nods.

It would explain why she held on to the house they once shared. But what I can't explain is how my grandmother's bottle of rare wine ended up in Malcolm's possession. An idea hits me. "When Autumn and I showed up at Sherry's house, she recognized me. I could see it on her face."

"Recognized you? I mean, I could see Malcolm mentioning you, but in order for her to recognize you, she must have been following Malcolm."

"No." I wish it were that simple, but it's much, much more disturbing. "Malcolm and I had never met in person, remember? Sherry had to look me up somehow."

"Do you still have that dating app on your phone?" he asks me.

"Yeah, why?"

"Because I want to see if there's a way to tell who views your profile."

I pull my phone out of my purse and click on the app before handing the phone to him.

His brow furrows. "I've never used one of these before. What do I do?"

"It's on my profile now. In the top right corner is my inbox. Any messages I get would be there."

"You don't have any," he says.

"That's probably because I marked myself as unavailable. It makes my profile inactive. I did it after I started talking to Malcolm."

"Does that mean people wouldn't be able to search you anymore?"

"I'm not sure."

"I think we need to contact the person in charge of this app."

"I have no idea who that is," I say. "My best friend convinced me to sign up for this. It's really not my thing at all."

"Tell you what. While you have your two o'clock appointment, I'll do some research into the app to find out who created it. If we can contact that person, we should be able to find out who viewed your profile."

"You mean find out if Sherry Monaghan viewed my profile to keep tabs on Malcolm."

"And we need to know how much information about you she might have been able to get a hold of in the process."

"You make it sound like she's going to come after me."

He hands me the phone back. "I don't want to scare you, but how do you know she won't?"

Chapter Twelve

Once my two o'clock appointment is over, I call Nolan. We exchanged numbers at the diner. I wouldn't say we're dating considering both meals we've shared revolved around discussing a murder case. It doesn't exactly spell romance. And I don't know if I'm ready to get my hopes up about any man at the current time. There's just too much going on.

The fact that I haven't heard from Detective Lange doesn't exactly put me at ease either. I know he's trying to build a case against me. If Sherry Monaghan really did kill her ex-husband and try to frame me, she'd be more than happy to help Drew Lange's investigation. He already knows I went to see her, and he might spin it to look like I went there to make sure Sherry didn't suspect me. Sherry would probably play right along to avoid being caught.

When Nolan doesn't answer, I decide not to leave a voice mail. "Where is he?" I ask aloud even though I'm in my office by myself.

There's a soft knock on my door, and then Lena walks in. "Did you call for me?"

I put my phone down on the desk and meet her gaze. "No, sorry. I was thinking aloud."

"I was about to head out for the day if you don't need anything."

"No, I'm fine. Thank you, Lena."

"I mailed the card to Randy as well. I hope you don't mind, but I read what you wrote in it. You're really good at knowing exactly what to say in any given situation."

Except for maybe with a certain police detective. I seem to only know how to rile him up and make him even more suspicious.

"Thanks," I say.

"All right, well, I'll see you in the morning." She closes the door behind her.

Since I can't get a hold of Nolan, I call Autumn. "Did everything dry up okay after yesterday's leak?" I ask when she picks up.

"Yeah, we're fine. We've got a big crowd of kids today." The after-school rush is usually like that. It's great that Autumn and Aaron are giving kids a safe place to go when there's no one at home for them. Not that most of these kids aren't old enough to stay home by themselves, but playing basketball or getting tutored after school keeps them out of trouble.

"I'm glad to hear it."

"How's the investigation going?" she asks.

I fill her in on what she's missed. "If Sherry did murder Malcolm, do you think the bank will take over the house and put it up for auction?"

"That's exactly what I've been wondering," I say with a sarcastic laugh.

"Sorry. I know you have bigger problems. I shouldn't keep bringing up my house hunting issues."

"Hey, your feelings and situation are equally as important as mine."

"Yeah, but you're facing possible jail time. I think that gives you the nod in this instance."

I take a deep breath. "I'm trying to get through to Nolan. We're supposed to meet up and figure out if Sherry viewed my Kindred Hearts profile."

"Be careful, Syd. This Sherry woman might be unhinged. Maybe you should call Detective Lange and tell him what you know. It might make him stop pointing the finger at you."

I doubt that. He's the type that can't admit when he's wrong. "He could probably catch Sherry with a smoking gun in her hand and somehow still find a way to blame me."

"It's crazy to think he and Nolan are related. They seem so different."

"They are."

She sighs through the phone. "I hate to say this, but are you sure you want to get involved with that family? I mean, let's say things work out with Nolan. You'd be stuck dealing with Drew for the rest of your life."

"I don't want to think about that right now. I only want to know where Nolan is." The skeptic in me is wondering if he set me up and pretended to be on my side but is feeding Drew information instead.

I shake my head. No. I would have been able to figure out they were acting. The feelings I saw between them at the diner were very real. They have an extremely strained relationship.

"Hey, I don't mean to cut you short, but I have someone at my door."

"Go. We'll talk later."

"Bye, Syd." She hangs up, and I open my laptop.

Even though I write by hand during my sessions, I always type up my notes into each patient's personal online file, adding my after-session impressions. I'm just finishing when my phone rings. I pick it up, noticing Nolan's name on the screen.

"Where have you been hiding?" I ask, saving my file.

"Sorry, I saw you tried to call. I was on the phone with my new boss. We were working out a few details before I start on Friday."

"You start on Friday? That seems a little strange."

"The news business is strange by nature. I do have some information for you." There's a shuffling sound on the other end. "Hang on. I had to print and sign some papers for work, and I buried the paper I wrote the woman's information on. It's here somewhere."

I'm really curious to know what his apartment looks like. He hasn't spoken very highly about it at all. I'm guessing it's tiny and cramped. And if I had to bet money on it, I'd say he's working off his kitchen table or coffee table because he doesn't have room for a desk.

"Found it." He exhales loudly. "Cynthia Snook started Kindred Hearts three years ago. She developed the app along with a small team. It seems like she was the brains behind the idea but didn't do much of the creation itself."

"I'm going to go out on a limb and say she doesn't live in Delaware."

"No, she's in California."

I won't be taking a road trip out there. "Did you happen to find a phone number for Kindred Hearts?"

"I did, and I got us a phone interview with her at four. I was thinking I could come to your office, and we could talk to her there."

"I'll text you the address," I tell him, opening my text messages and typing away.

"You do know I'm an investigative reporter, right? I'm pretty sure I could have found your address on my own."

"Yes, but it's way less creepy when I give it to you instead of you researching me."

"I didn't think of it that way, but now that you say it, I'm starting to see where I've gone wrong with women in the past." He laughs.

"I'm going to tell myself that was a joke. See you soon." I hang up, but I'm still smiling.

I finish up for the day and pick up the novel I keep in my bottom drawer for when I have downtime.

Nolan knocks on my office door as I'm flipping a page.

"Come in," I say, placing my magnetic bookmark in my spot and returning the book to the drawer.

Nolan looks around the office. "I was expecting nothing more than a couch and chair."

"You watch too much TV," I say.

My office does have a couch and chair, but I also have a play area for children, a large bean bag chair—popular with my teenage patients—and a desk with chairs. I want my patients to sit wherever they're most comfortable.

"Your view is nice, too. Doesn't that distract people, though?"

"More like soothes." One wall is mostly windows overlooking a lake. Right now, a heron is standing on the water's edge. "Herbert is very nonjudgmental."

"Herbert?" Nolan asks.

I get up and walk to the window. "He's right down there. He spends most of his day by the lake. My patients seem to like him." I had one young girl who used to talk to Herbert instead of me. I didn't mind because she was still opening up about her feelings. Lucy and her family moved away about four months ago. I still miss her.

Nolan looks at his watch. "Where do you want to sit to make the call?"

"Your choice," I say, motioning to all the available seating options.

He eyes me suspiciously. "I feel like this is a test. Are you going to analyze me based on where I choose to sit?"

"Totally. The couch means you're comfortable with me. The desk and chairs keep distance between us. The bean bag is just odd and selfish because it would leave no room for me other than the floor. And the play area, well that would tell me you never grew up."

His mouth hangs open. "Maybe meeting here was a bad idea."

I laugh. "I'm teasing. I made all that up off the top of my head."

"Still, you choose," he says.

"Indecisive. Interesting."

He looks like he's about to run from the office.

"I'm kidding. You're way too easy to mess with. To be honest, I've sat in every chair in this room. They're all comfortable."

"Which is your favorite?" he asks.

I smirk. "Honestly, the play area. That foam mat is really comfortable, and it has the best view of the lake. But if this is going to be a video call, I'm thinking we should steer clear of it."

"Good point. Couch?"

I nod and walk over to it. Nolan sits beside me and takes out his phone. "I did request a video call because I thought it might be helpful for you to see her reactions to our questions."

"You really do think I analyze people twenty-four seven, don't you?"

"I think most people do," he says.

"You're not wrong there."

He makes the call, and it starts ringing on the other end. After three rings, a blonde woman with glasses answers. I'd guess she's about fifty years old.

"Mrs. Snook, hello," Nolan says.

"It's Ms.," she corrects him, which I immediately find odd. Here's a woman who makes a living from an app meant to help people find love, and she herself is single.

"My apologies."

"No need. I'm single by choice. You must be Detective Lange."

I whip my head in Nolan's direction, and it takes all my might to keep my mouth shut. He's pretending to be his brother! Impersonating a police officer is a felony.

"This is Dr. Sydney Warner. We'd like to speak to you about Sydney's profile on your app."

"Is there a problem with your profile?" she asks me.

"I'm not sure. I'm trying to find out who has viewed it. I'm hoping you can help me with that."

"I see. Since the police are involved, I'm assuming you've been threatened in some way."

Threatened to be thrown in jail for murder, yes. I nod.

"Well, as you probably know since you're a user yourself, the app is designed to allow people to be anonymous until they decide they want to be seen."

"What exactly does that mean?" Nolan asks her.

"It means that anyone who is a member can view other member's profiles."

"So no profile is ever private, even when it's considered inactive?" he asks.

"That's correct."

"What about on your end?" I ask. "Can you see who is doing what?"

"Me personally, no. I'm afraid this app is my creation in the sense that I came up with the idea for it. As for how it actually works, I had nothing to do with that. I'm not a technology person. I'm a matchmaker. I couldn't compete with the digital age, so I found people who could take my ideas and make them into a usable app for people to connect."

"Would those creators be able to see which users were viewing my profile?" I ask.

"Yes, or at least, I would assume so."

"Great. We're going to need you to get them on that task, and we're also going to need you to find out who was viewing Malcolm Monaghan's profile as well."

"I'd be happy to assist Dr. Warner with her own account, but I'm afraid looking into another user's personal information is against our privacy policy."

"Malcolm Monaghan is dead. He was murdered last Friday night," Nolan says.

"Oh, my." She looks away from the camera. "Are you thinking the murderer used my app to commit this heinous crime?"

"I'm afraid so," Nolan says, "which is why I'm sure you can understand why we'd like your assistance."

He's still letting her believe he's a police detective. While he never actually came out and confirmed it in words, he never corrected her either. Is that the same thing? I'm sure if Drew finds out, he'll believe it is. I can see him charging his own brother with a felony.

"I'll need some time. Is this a good number to get back to you?" she asks.

"Yes. Thank you. We really appreciate your cooperation in this investigation."

"Of course. I admit I'm crossing my fingers that my IT guys don't find anything, though. This is not what I created the app for."

"We understand," Nolan says. "Thank you for your time." He ends the call.

"What were you thinking, letting her believe you're a police detective?" I ask.

He holds up a hand. "I never said I was Drew. I gave her my real name. She must have tried to look me up and somehow got me confused with Drew."

Andrew and Nolan are not names you mix up. Unless the person who scheduled the meeting only remembered the last name and mentioned an investigation. I could see how that would lead Cynthia Snook to assume it was Detective Lange who had requested the appointment.

"You should have corrected her," I say.

"I know that, but I also know she didn't have to talk to us."

"I'm one of her clients. If I asked her to look into my account, she'd have to do it."

"Yes, but what about Malcolm's? If someone was stalking both of your profiles, it has to be the killer. This is our best shot at finding them."

I know he's right, but my moral compass still isn't satisfied.

"Look, if I had the kind of big brother I could go to for help, I would have asked Drew to call her for the information."

Instead, that big brother is intent on finding a way to arrest me without the necessary evidence.

"Okay, but if she calls you Detective Lange again, you have to correct her." It's a moot point considering she most likely will have already given us the information we need by then, but it makes me feel a little better to insist upon it.

"Deal. Now, do you have dinner plans?"

"Nolan, I don't think that's a good idea." I stand up and walk to the window.

"Because I misled Cynthia Snook?" he says from his seat on the couch.

I turn to face him. "You're also Drew's brother."

"I get it." He stands up. "Tell you what. Let me help you solve this case, and once it's over, I'll ask you to dinner again. If you still don't want to go, I'll back off."

I'm surprised he still wants to help me after I rejected him. Maybe he is a good guy after all. "Deal."

Chapter Thirteen

Tuesday morning, I'm seated in my office with a cup of coffee in my hand and my air pods in as I talk to Autumn.

"I still can't believe you turned him down. You signed up for that app because you were tired of being alone, Syd. Then you meet a great guy like Nolan, and you push him away."

"He's Drew's brother. You said it yourself. That's weird. And especially now with the investigation going on. I don't want to talk about it."

"The therapist is clamming up and not wanting to talk about her feelings?" She tsks into the phone. "Fine. But let me say this. Not going out with Nolan when you clearly like him is the same thing as letting Drew win."

"No, it's not."

"Oh, really? You don't think he wants you two to stop seeing each other?" she challenges.

I exhale loudly. "It's not the same thing, though. Not really."

"Keep telling yourself that. My guess is you'll see Nolan today at some point. Despite your protests, you'll continue to see him under the guise of working this case."

"That is what we're doing. There's no disguising anything."

"You know, Syd, you're very good at figuring out other people, but when it comes to yourself, you can be so completely clueless."

Lena knocks on my door and opens it. "Billy Danvers is here for his appointment."

"Send him in," I tell her. "Autumn, I have to go. My first appointment is here."

"Good luck," she says and hangs up.

Billy is a bean bag person, so I wheel my desk chair over near the bean bag. Billy's a sophomore in high school. His parents decided to homeschool him after he was bullied throughout middle school.

"Hi," he says in a quiet voice as he enters my office.

"Good morning, Billy. Can I offer you a drink?" I have a mini fridge I keep stocked with my patients' favorite drinks.

"No, I'm good. I had a big breakfast."

"What's on your mind today?" I ask.

"Death."

That's a new topic for him. "What about it?"

"I saw the newspaper article about that guy. You found him, right?"

"I did," I say.

"I've never seen a dead body. What did it look like?"

I'm not sure how happy his parents will be if he tells them I described Malcolm's dead body to him. "Why do you ask?"

"I realized I don't know what a dead person looks like. I mean I've seen movies, but you know those are dramatized."

I nod. "Most people are afraid of dying, which makes the sight of a dead person disturbing to them."

"Growing up, my parents always told me death wasn't a scary thing. It's a natural part of life."

"It can be." Murder isn't natural, though.

"I was wondering if a dead body really looks all that much different from someone who's asleep."

"It would depend upon how the person died."

"Yeah, I guess you're right." He's quiet for a minute. I've learned to let Billy have his quiet moments. It means he's working out how to ask the question on his mind. I take the time to jot down some notes in my notebook.

"When my grandfather died, I wasn't allowed to go to the funeral."

"Why not?"

"It was an open casket, and my parents thought it would upset me. Do you know what really upset me?"

"What?"

"Not getting to say goodbye to my granddad."

"You wish you'd gotten to attend the funeral?"

He nods. "The day of the funeral, they sent me to school. They said I should keep busy and go on with life as usual."

They basically told him to ignore his feelings all together. That's never good.

"I just wanted to go with them. I was angry at first. I sat through my classes and refused to talk when the teachers called on me. And as the day went on, my anger turned to sadness. I broke down and cried when my health teacher started talking about reproduction. Everyone thought it was the topic that made me upset. I was so humiliated. I ran out of class and stayed in the bathroom until one of the security guards found me and brought me to the nurse. That's when the bullying started."

"Did you ever tell your parents what happened?"

He nods. "My dad told me everyone gets embarrassed at some point in school. He told me to ignore them, but every day it got worse and worse. Finally, my mom pulled me out and started homeschooling me."

"You've never told me this before."

"Everyone always made death seem like something you can't talk about."

"You can talk about anything and everything you want to in here."

"I know. You're cool, Doc. You don't judge me."

"You want to know a secret?" I ask him, leaning forward in my chair.

He laces his hands behind his head and leans back in the bean bag. "Yeah."

"Not a person on this planet has a clue what they're doing. No matter how old they are. Some are just better at pretending they do. But if you want to be happy in life, all you have to do is realize that you're allowed to feel however you feel at any given moment. No one can tell you your feelings are wrong."

"But they do tell me."

"And does that change how you feel?" I ask.

"No."

"Exactly. Your feelings aren't wrong. Others might disagree with them, but that's their opinion, which also isn't wrong. They're entitled to those feelings, too."

"How can no one be wrong?"

"We all act differently in certain situations. For instance, when you see someone get hurt, do you cringe or find humor in it?"

"Depends if they're badly hurt or not. I wouldn't laugh at someone who gets really hurt, but if they trip or something small and I know they're okay, I might laugh."

"And some others might laugh because they're nervous. Or scared. Or don't know how to act in the moment."

"So it's the reason that's more important than the action?" he asks.

"Yes. And the reason is rooted in the person's emotions, right?"

"I guess so. And that would mean every one of those reactions is okay?"

I nod.

"What about people who like to see other people hurt? Don't they exist?"

"They do. And that's why some people wind up murdered, like the man you saw on the news."

"Aren't they wrong?" Billy asks. "Their emotions, I mean?"

"Again, it depends. If someone kills another person because they felt betrayed or hurt by them, those feelings of hurt aren't wrong, but the action that followed them is."

"Then we're entitled to feel however we feel, but how we act on those feelings can be wrong."

"You're a smart kid, Billy." I smile at him.

"Some people are saying you killed that man, but I know you wouldn't hurt another human being. You're too good a person, Doc Warner."

"I consider that very high praise coming from you, Billy."

Once my morning sessions are over, I check my phone for missed calls and messages. Nolan sent me a "Call me as soon as you can" message, so I dial his number.

"Sydney, hey. Are you at the office?" he asks.

"Yeah. I'm on my lunch break. Why?"

"Any chance you can cancel your afternoon sessions?"

"What for? What's going on?"

"It's Gerard Cowen. He called me. He wants us to come to the college. He has something big to tell us and doesn't want to do it over the phone."

I look at my appointment book even though I already know who I'm supposed to see this afternoon. "Maybe I can do a phone session. Let me call my patient and try to switch it."

"I'm on my way to your office to pick you up."

It must be really important if Nolan is so insistent. I wonder if Gerard sounded like he was in trouble. I get on the phone and call Marla Erikson. Luckily, she's okay with doing a phone session. I don't mention I'll be in the car with Nolan, and since I already have her on the phone, I offer her more time by talking to her now through my lunch break. The offer appeases her.

When Nolan arrives, I scribble a note to Lena, who is out on her lunch break, so she'll know where I am when she gets back. Since Marla was my last client of the day, I also tell Lena to take the rest of the day off with pay. Nolan picks up on the fact that I'm already on my phone session, and he's careful not to let on that he's with me.

We walk to his car and get in. It takes almost an hour to drive to the college, mostly because there was an accident on Route One that we had to wait to be cleared. That means my session with Marla is finished before we arrive.

"Sorry about that," I say after ending the call.

"Don't apologize. I'm sorry I had to pull you away from work like that, but Gerard Cowen was very insistent that we come right away. He sounded scared for his life."

"Why didn't he call the police?" I ask.

"He said he did. He spoke to my brother, and as soon as Gerard mentioned our names, Drew was sure we'd put him up to it to get him off your scent."

I can't believe this. "When he turns out to be wrong about me, he's going to get in big trouble with the SCPD."

"I don't know. Drew can be pretty convincing. If I didn't know him the way I do, I might have believed the evidence he's stacking against you."

"That makes me feel so much better," I say, my tone full of sarcasm.

"Sorry, but you should know what you're up against. Drew is ruthless when he thinks he's putting a criminal behind bars, and right now, he believes you are that criminal."

"I can't prove I didn't know about the bottle of wine, but he can't prove I did either."

"Possession is nine-tenths of the law, though."

"Isn't that rule meant to help people establish ownership, not place blame on people?" I ask.

"It works both ways. We're here." He pulls up a long driveway that leads to the main building on campus. You wouldn't think this was a college by the looks of it. There are plenty of buildings and athletic fields. I remember reading that at one time, this was a military training facility.

Nolan parks. "Gerard's office is on the third floor of this building here."

I'm not sure if Gerard told him that or if he looked it up. Not that it matters much. I just want to know what's got Gerard so scared.

Nolan pulls a reporter's badge from his jacket. "I picked this up from work today. I might not start until Friday, but college security won't know that. Hopefully, this will get us inside if anyone tries to stop us."

"I'm pretty sure Gerard Cowen will vouch for us. We have an appointment to see him, don't we?" I ask.

"Yeah, that too. But it doesn't hurt to be on the safe side."

I guess I should be happy his plan wasn't to portray his detective brother this time. I still haven't completely gotten over that lie.

We find the psychology department offices located in the center of the third floor. We walk, and there's no one at the front desk.

"Did Gerard tell you where his office is?"

"He's department head now, so I say we look for the largest office, probably in a corner."

I nod, and we walk past the closed doors down the first hallway. I'm about to suggest the end door when I realize the hallway turns to the left, and at the end of that row of doors is a plaque that reads "Department Head." "There," I tell him. As I get closer, I see it's still Malcolm's name underneath the words "Department Head," but I'm certain Gerard will be inside.

Nolan knocks. "It's Nolan Lange and Dr. Sydney Warner," he says.

The door is practically thrown open. Gerard Cowen looks like he was wrestling a wild coyote. His hair is disheveled, his tie is undone, and his shirt is partially unbuttoned. "Did anyone follow you?" he asks, ushering us into the office. He quickly closes the door and locks it behind us.

"No. Professor Cowen, what is going on?" I ask.

"It was that student. Emmett Michaelson. He showed up at my office this morning to plead with me to read his paper and give him a better grade."

"You mean he showed up at Malcolm's office," I say.

"This is my office now. Anyway, I told him I have to uphold all of Professor Monaghan's grades but that I'd be grading all assignments from this point forward."

"How did he react to that?" Nolan asks.

"Like I'd personally failed him. He threatened me. Said he'd go to the dean and have me fired if I didn't give him a higher grade."

Which he can't actually do, so it's an empty threat. "What else?" He's too spooked for that to be all that happened.

He pulls a paper from the top drawer of his desk. "I found this slid under my door after my last class." He hands the paper to me.

I read it aloud, "'Change the grade or I'll personally see to it that you meet the same fate Professor Monaghan did.'" I look up at Gerard. "Did you tell Detective Lange about this?"

"He wouldn't listen to me."

"You have to go to the police with this. He's threatening your life. This is proof."

"I have no proof Emmett wrote it," Gerard says. "I've never even seen his handwriting, and even if they bring him into the station and force him to write something, he'll know why he's there, and he can alter his handwriting."

He's right. Unless someone saw Emmett slip the note under the door, we can't prove he was the one who wrote it.

"There's only one thing to do," I say.

"What?" Nolan looks at me.

"We need to bring this note to Emmett and force a confession out of him."

"How do you plan to do that? If he killed Malcolm and is threatening to kill Gerard, there's nothing to say he won't try to kill us."

"I know."

Chapter Fourteen

Gerard Cowen just stares at Nolan and me. "Do you two know what you're doing? If this guy really killed Malcolm…" He flops down into his desk chair. "We need the authorities. I'm going to call campus police. Maybe they'll listen." He picks up his phone.

I can't stop him, nor do I want to. Going to see Emmett alone is not the smartest idea I've ever had. I'm in way over my head. And while I'm not a huge fan of Gerard Cowen, the man is clearly scared for his life right now. He's realized getting what he wanted came at a huge price. He never hated Malcolm enough to want him dead. And the fact that he got Malcolm's course load that way will stay with him forever. I wouldn't be surprised if he leaves First State and finds a teaching position elsewhere to put all of this behind him.

But right now, all any of us can do is try to find Emmett. Campus police will be able to look up where Emmett lives. Gerard's phone call doesn't take long, and once he's finished, he laces his fingers on his desk and takes a few deep breaths. "Campus police are on their way. Emmett rooms on campus, so they'll get the note, ask me a few questions, and then go talk to him."

"There's on-campus housing?" Nolan asks, and I get why he didn't think there would be since the campus isn't exactly that large.

Gerard nods. "There are four on-campus housing buildings for students. As far as small colleges go, First State is among the top of the list in academics." His tone is full of sorrow, confirming my suspicion that Gerard won't stay at First State for long after this.

"I'm sorry," I say, wanting him to know someone understands how he feels right now.

He meets my gaze. "Why are you two so invested in this case? Neither of you is law enforcement. Why not let the police handle this?"

"Because they're looking in the wrong direction," I say. I'm not going to get into the details with him.

There's a knock on the office door. "Campus police," says a deep male voice.

Gerard gets up and opens the door to let two police officers inside. "Thank you for coming."

The male officer is tall and thin, and beside him is a female officer, who looks like she's ready to lay down the law. She's easily twice as intimidating as he is.

"Where's the threatening letter?" the female officer asks, holding out her hand.

Gerard gives it to her. "I believe a student by the name of Emmett Michaelson left it for me."

"Michaelson?" the male officer asks. I squint to read the name embroidered on his jacket. Officer Casey. "Isn't he on the baseball team?"

"Yes," I say. "Do you know him?"

"He's the star pitcher," Officer Casey says. "My kid loves him. We go to every game Michaelson pitches."

Then Emmett absolutely missed hitting Malcolm's window with that rock on purpose. He was warning him. I'm not sure I think this guy is capable of murder, unless he finally snapped.

"Could we accompany you to Michaelson's dorm room?" I ask.

The female officer, Officer Darling, according to her jacket, crosses her arms. Her name is the antithesis of the feelings she puts off. There's nothing darling about this woman. She's fierce. "Why would you want to come with us?"

"I'm a psychologist. I'm very good at reading people. I think I could be of some help. I already know the history Emmett Michaelson has with his psychology grade and his professors."

"And I'm a reporter," Nolan says. "I interview people for a living."

"Okay, but we'll handle the questions," Officer Darling says.

I'm fine with that as long as we get to tag along.

We follow the officers across campus to the quad. There are four dorms positioned around the common area. They're all identical. Officer Darling brings us to the one that butts up against the fitness center.

"This is Metzgar Hall. Michaelson rooms on the second floor." Officer Darling uses a key card to enter the building. I'm sure it's a universal key to get her into any building on campus.

The front desk is manned by a college student. She's reading and only looks up at us briefly before getting back to her book. I guess she doesn't need to ask us for any identification since we're with two campus police officers.

We take the elevator to the second floor and follow Officer Darling straight down the hallway to our right when we get off the elevator. "Here we are. Room 212." She knocks. "Campus Police."

I'm not sure that's the best way to get a college student to open their door. Officer Darling's universal key card isn't going to work on this door, which uses a regular key for entry. If Emmett is inside, he could be quiet and pretend he's not there.

"Emmett Michaelson," Officer Darling calls. "Open up."

No one answers the door.

"We'll have to try to contact him another way," Officer Casey says. "He must be in class or at practice right now."

"Can't you easily check his schedule?" I ask.

"We could, but I'm not about to pull him out of class when we have no proof he's done anything wrong," Officer Darling says.

"We understand," Nolan says, reaching for my elbow. "Come on, Sydney. I'm sure these officers are more than capable of handling this from here."

I'm about to protest and ask him what's come over him, when I see the subtle widening of his eyes. He doesn't actually mean what he's saying. "Of course. Officers, thank you for your help, and good luck from here." I nod to each of them before walking back down the hallway.

When we get to the elevator, I press the button. I don't plan on walking away. I'm not leaving here without answers. "I want to stay. Emmett has to come back at some point," I tell Nolan once we're in the elevator alone.

"If we leave the dorm, we'll need someone to let us back inside."

"Then we won't leave the dorm," I say.

The elevator doors open on the ground floor, and I start past the mailboxes to a door on the opposite end of the building that I'm hoping leads to the stairwell. I push the door and smile when I see the stairs. I climb to the second floor and stop on the landing. The door to the floor doesn't have a window in it, so I have no way of knowing if the campus police have left yet. I sit down on the top stair.

"What's the plan?" Nolan asks.

"I thought you had one with the way you were trying to get me to leave with you back there."

"I wish. I just knew we couldn't stay with them."

They weren't completely unhelpful. They did get us inside the dorm. Of course, they also took the note, and without it, I won't be able to see how Emmett reacts to it. I'm losing the advantage I have when it comes to reading people's emotions and body language. But it's not like I could argue with Officer Darling. She has the authority to look into this matter. I don't.

"If we wait long enough, Emmett will have to come back to his room. We can corner him and find out the truth."

"Are you really that good at telling when someone is lying?" he asks me.

"It's easier when I know the person. People can have different tells."

"Tells?"

"Yeah, clues that they're not being truthful. Some people's voices go up in pitch. Others can't make eye contact. Some squirm."

"So you're like a human lie detector."

"Not exactly. Some people are quite skilled at hiding their emotions, and that makes it difficult for me to pick up on whether or not they're lying."

"Is that like how some people can fool lie detector tests?" he asks.

I bob my head. We've waited long enough to take a peek and see if Officers Darling and Casey have left, so I stand up and walk to the door. I open it enough to see down the hallway. I don't see either officer, but there is a girl going into the room next to Emmett's. "Come on," I tell Nolan, swinging the door open and starting toward the girl.

She makes it inside her room before I can reach her, so I have to knock. Nolan doesn't ask what I'm doing, which means he's either figured it out on his own, or he's willing to follow my lead. I raise my hand and knock on the girl's door.

"Would you stop stalking my door, Emmett?" the girl says, swinging the door open and glaring at me. Her eyes widen when she realizes I'm not who she thought I'd be.

"I'm sorry to bother you, but we were hoping to talk to you about your neighbor, Emmett Michaelson."

"What about him?" she asks, leaning on the doorframe.

"Could we maybe come inside?"

She looks Nolan and me up and down. "No offense but I don't know you. You're not exactly young enough to go to school here either, so I think I'll talk to you right here where other people can see us."

I turn to look at Nolan, trying to determine if he's thinking the same thing I am. She has drugs in her room, and she's afraid we're narcs. "Is that why Emmett watches to see when you come home?" I ask.

"Is what why? I don't know what you're talking about." She shifts uncomfortably on her feet.

"We aren't here to bust you for drugs," I say. "We want to talk to Emmett, but he doesn't seem to be around."

"He's probably at practice. Have you tried the baseball field?"

That's most likely where the campus police went next. "Not yet. How well do you know Emmett?"

"Not well. We don't talk much."

I'm guessing they have more of a business relationship. "Doesn't the school drug test their athletes?" I ask.

"You're the only one who's said anything about drugs." She crosses her arms, getting defensive.

I have to change tactics before she slams the door in our faces. "I was under the impression he used drugs. I figured you might have known. That's all. Did you happen to know he was having a hard time with his psychology class?"

She shakes her head. "Like I said, we don't really talk. Sorry." She backs up into her room and closes the door behind her. Then I hear the click of a lock slipping into place.

"She's a little shady," Nolan says.

"Yeah, well, drug dealers usually get that way."

"You think she's Emmett's dealer?" Nolan's eyes widen. "That tiny girl?"

I nod. "She was defensive, felt Nolan always watched her door, and said they didn't talk much. I'm convinced he buys drugs from her."

"Well, okay then. Now what?"

"I think we should wait for Nolan's roommate."

"Why not go to the baseball field like the girl said?"

"Because I'm guessing that's what the campus police did. I'd rather they think we left."

"We're going to look suspicious hanging around outside Emmett's door, though. Someone on the floor might call campus police to have us removed."

I look around. The only one we know is home is the girl we just talked to, and there's no way she's going to call the campus police and risk getting busted for having drugs in her room. "I think we're safe, at least for a little while."

We aren't old enough to pass for parents of anyone who goes here, but we won't blend in as students either. I try to think of a plausible excuse for being here that won't draw suspicion, but I come up empty-handed.

"What if we claim we're relatives? Older cousins or aunt and uncle maybe?" Nolan suggests.

"I guess that could work if anyone asks." I sit down outside Emmett's door. "Sometimes, I still can't believe this is all happening. I mean four days ago, I naively thought I was about to meet a nice guy. Now I find out he was secretly dating his ex-wife, was trying to evade an angry student, and wasn't at all the man I thought he was."

"It's hard to meet people these days. Anyone can be anyone else online." Nolan sits down beside me and gently squeezes my knee. "Don't be so hard on yourself. You might have better insight into the human mind than most people do, but you're still human yourself." He's right. It's so easy for judgement to be clouded by what you want to be true.

"Thanks for listening to me."

"I'm guessing you're used to providing a listening ear for others, but you probably aren't used to having someone do it for you."

"My best friend, Autumn, is great for that. She's been busy at the youth center trying to fix things after they had a leaky pipe over the weekend."

"Autumn, that name sounds familiar."

"She's Autumn Young now, but in school she was Autumn Walker. We met because our last names were close in the alphabet, and we usually got seated next to each other in class because of it."

"Ah, the dreaded old alphabetical seating."

"Why did you dread it?" I ask. "Your last name falls in the middle of the alphabet, so it's not like you were always seated upfront like the As."

"No, but anything based on last names meant I was immediately compared to Drew."

"I'm sorry."

"I've dealt with it for thirty-one years now. I'll live." He bumps his shoulder into mine.

The elevator doors open, and a guy comes walking toward us. He pauses as he gets closer. "Can I help you?"

Nolan and I both stand up.

"Do you live here?" I ask, motioning to room 212.

"Yeah. Why?"

"Are you Emmett Michaelson?" Nolan asks.

The guy shakes his head. "He's my roommate. I'm Paul."

"Hi, Paul." I can't exactly tell him we're Emmett's relatives now that Nolan asked the guy if he was Emmett. That cover is completely blown. "Would we be able to come inside and ask you a few questions about Emmett?"

Paul looks frightened by the idea. "I don't think Emmett would like that very much."

"Is he expected back soon?" Nolan asks.

Paul looks at his phone in his hand. "No. He should be at practice now, and then he usually goes to dinner with the guys on his team."

"Then he doesn't have to know about this," Nolan says with a smile.

"What's this about?" Paul asks, looking at me. "Did Emmett do something?"

"What makes you ask that?" Nolan says.

Paul looks all around the hallway before whispering, "Because I think he might have killed someone."

Chapter Fifteen

Paul is terrified of his roommate. That much is clear. And Emmett must have made his feelings for Malcolm very known for Paul to jump to the conclusion that Emmett killed someone. I'm sure Paul heard about Malcolm's death. I'm guessing everyone on campus knows about it. Schools are the biggest rumor mills around.

"You want to get away from Emmett, don't you, Paul?" I say, placing a comforting hand on his arm.

He nods.

"We might be able to help you, but you need to let us inside your dorm room."

He swallows so hard I hear it. His hand shakes as he unlocks the door. He quickly shuts the door behind us. "If he comes back while you're here, you have to pretend we're related and you're just visiting."

"If anyone asks, we can say we're your cousins," Nolan suggests.

Paul nods and puts his backpack down on the bed closest to the door. "That's Emmett's bed there. And that's his desk and closet."

It's like he's giving us permission to search Emmett's belongings.

"How long have you and Emmett been roommates?" I ask.

"Student housing paired us at the start of the school year. I'd never met him before that. We both had different roommates last year, but they didn't work out." Paul lowers his gaze to the floor.

"Can I ask what happened?"

Paul shrugs. "I turned him in for cheating. I found a bunch of tests on his laptop. I don't know how he got a hold of them, but he was selling copies to other students. It wound up being a big mess, and he was expelled."

I can imagine. "It must have been difficult for you," I say, automatically slipping into therapist mode. I can't control it sometimes. I have an undeniable need to let people know I understand how they feel.

He bobs his head. "I was scared. I mean, Ian wasn't a big guy or anything, but you never know what people are capable of."

He's right about that. And now his current roommate might be a murderer. Poor Paul.

"What makes you think Emmett committed murder?" I ask.

Paul motions to Emmett's desk but doesn't move even a step toward it. "He has these notes on one of his professors. Like he was watching him all the time."

"Where are they?" Nolan asks, moving toward the desk.

"That composition notebook there."

I wouldn't have guessed Emmett was old school and wrote things down instead of putting the information in his phone.

Nolan picks up the notebook and opens it. I stand next to him to view it at the same time. He flips through the pages first without reading them. Almost half the notebook is full.

He goes back to the beginning and starts reading. It's mostly dates, times, and locations.

"There's no mention of Malcolm," I say.

"Do you mean Professor Monaghan?" Paul asks.

I nod. "Did you know him?"

"I had him last semester. He's tough. Emmett was struggling. He said he'd be doing fine if he'd gotten Professor Cowen instead. I guess Professor Monaghan wouldn't allow him to drop the class either."

"Did he talk about Professor Monaghan a lot?" Nolan asks.

"He yelled more than talked. He said the man was out to ruin him. Emmett can't afford to go to school here without his scholarship. And I've seen the classes he takes. They're all super easy and entry level. I don't think he's here for the education. He only came to college to keep playing ball. If he loses that, I'm guessing he'll drop out."

"Is Emmett aware that you know this notebook exists?" I ask.

Paul shrugs. "I didn't say anything to him about it. After last year, I don't want to be responsible for another student getting kicked out of school, and I don't want Emmett coming after me, either. Not when…" He swallows hard and sits down on his bed. "Am I in danger?"

I'm not sure how to answer that.

"Has Emmett ever threatened you?" Nolan asks.

"No, but I'm thinking that would change if he found out I know about the notebook."

It would probably change if Emmett found out Paul let us into their room. We have to make sure we're not in here when Emmett returns.

"Did you suspect him immediately when you found out Professor Monaghan was dead?" I ask.

Paul nods. "Emmett was so happy when we heard. There was a story on our campus news channel. We watched it together, and I swear he smiled through the whole thing."

"Why haven't you requested a room change?" Nolan asks. "You must be afraid to share a room with him at this point."

"I am, but I figure I'm safer if he doesn't know what I suspect. If I leave…"

"He'll question why," I say.

"Yeah, and my parents live too far for me to commute back and forth every day."

"Could you request a single room with no roommate and play it off as needing the quiet to study? Maybe pretend your grades are suffering and your parents are insisting on a single room so you can be more focused and get your grades up?" I suggest.

Paul considers it for a moment. "That's not bad. It might work. I can tell Emmett my parents and I got into a big argument over it. I should go to the student housing office right now and find out if there are any single rooms available. They cost more, though. I'm not sure my parents are going to be happy about that part."

"It can't hurt to talk to them." I look at the notebook in Nolan's hands. "Nolan, flip to the last entry Emmett made. What does it say?"

He turns the pages, coming to rest on the final one with writing on it. "Oh, boy." He lets out a deep breath, and I read over his shoulder.

Friday: dismissed class early. Big date for Valentine's Day. Park. Willow Tree.

"This is evidence," I say. "He knew about Malcolm's date with me. He knew where it was going to be."

"We need to bring this to the police," Nolan says.

"You can't!" Paul shrieks. "He'll kill me."

"Paul, the police are going to arrest him," Nolan says. "This is the proof we need that shows Emmett had both motive and means to kill Professor Monaghan."

Paul's eyes widen. "You have to leave. I won't admit to letting you in here. I'll deny it. I'll tell them you must have broken in."

"You're going to lie to police officers?" I ask. "Paul, think about this. If you lie and the police find out about it, they're going to look at you as an accomplice to murder. Is that what you really want?" I feel bad for scaring him more, but he has to help us. This is our chance to get Emmett.

"Come with us to the campus police," Nolan says. "If you tell them what you found, they'll protect you. They'll get you out of this room."

"At no extra charge for a single," I tell him, hoping that will sway him to cooperate with us.

Paul thinks it over for a few seconds. "Do I pack first?" He looks around in a complete panic.

"No, just come with us."

I take the notebook from Nolan. "We have to bring this."

It takes Paul a few more seconds to even stand up.

"Paul, we're going to be right there with you. I promise we won't let anything happen to you," I say.

He looks like he's about to be sick, so I take him by the arm.

The door to the room opens, and I immediately shove the notebook inside my jacket.

"Emmett," Paul says, and his entire body goes rigid. I'm afraid he's going to pass out.

I have to think quickly. "Paul, this is your roommate?" I ask. "Hi, we're Paul's aunt and uncle."

Emmett barely even looks at us, going to his bed and searching under it. "Have you seen my mitt?" he asks Paul. "I brought the wrong one to practice. I need my lucky mitt. The new one isn't broken in, and I keep missing catches."

When Paul doesn't answer, I discreetly shake his arm.

"No," Paul manages to say.

"We should get going, or we'll be late for our dinner reservation," Nolan says. "Come on, Paul." He waves us on.

"It was nice to meet you," I say to Emmett as I push Paul from the room.

We take the elevator because I'm not sure Paul could handle walking down the stairs at the moment. Once the doors close with us inside, he practically starts hyperventilating. "He's going to know. He's going to know."

"Paul, try to calm down," Nolan says.

"He's busy searching for his baseball mitt. That should buy us time," I say.

"Why is baseball already practicing anyway?" Nolan asks. "It seems early for spring sports."

"It's not official practice. The guys on his team get together to play. The coach isn't there."

I don't really care about sports practices right now. I want to get this notebook to the campus police. "Paul, do you know where the campus police are located?" I ask as we get out of the elevator.

"Yeah. They're over by the registrar building."

"Good. Let's go."

We follow him across campus. With every step we get farther away from the dorm and Emmett, the more Paul seems to feel at ease. We open the door to the campus police building, and I spot Officer Darling. Her eyes narrow when she sees us.

"You're still here?" she asks, marching over to us.

"We've been talking to Paul here. He's Emmett Michaelson's roommate." I place my hand on Paul's arm, partially to make sure he doesn't chicken out and try to run off.

"Did you manage to find Emmett?" Nolan asks them.

"No, we got a call about a disturbance in one of the dorms. We had to make that a priority."

That's probably a good thing because Emmett might have been suspicious if the police had cornered him on the baseball field.

"Paul discovered this in Emmett's belongings," I say, pulling the notebook from my jacket. "He's afraid his roommate was watching Professor Monaghan and might have had something to do with what happened last Friday night."

Officer Darling takes the notebook and scans the contents. Still reading, she says, "Follow me." She brings us to her desk, and she sits down. "This belongs to Emmett?" she asks Paul.

"Yes, ma'am. Officer Ma'am," Paul fumbles.

She nods to him. "When did you find this?"

Paul looks like he's about to cry.

"Paul, tell Officer Darling about the news coverage of Professor Monaghan's death," I say.

Paul sinks into the chair in front of Officer Darling's desk. "I turned on the news, and they were talking about what happened to Professor Monaghan. Emmett was in his bed on his phone, but he stopped whatever he was doing and watched the news segment. He smiled. He was happy to hear Professor Monaghan was dead."

"Did it seem like it was the first he was hearing about Professor Monaghan's death?" Officer Darling asks.

"I-I don't know. He was so calm. He didn't seem all that surprised, though."

"And when did you discover this notebook?" she repeats since Paul never answered that question.

"About a week ago. I knew Emmett was having trouble with Monaghan's class. He was always talking about how Monaghan had it out for him."

"Did he seem agitated when he spoke about Professor Monaghan?" she asks him.

Paul nods. "He'd come home sometimes and go straight to his desk to write in that notebook. I didn't know what it was at first, but then he left it open one day. He rushed out of the room like he suddenly remembered something. I thought it might be something bad, so I went over to the open notebook and saw what was written in it."

"What did you think at that point?" she asks.

"I thought maybe Emmett was trying to keep track of Professor Monaghan's schedule so he could corner him about his grade some more. You know, try to wear him down." He looks down at his lap. "But after the news story, I thought maybe he was following him and learning his schedule for another reason."

"Officer Darling, Paul would like a new room assignment for his own safety," I say.

Paul nods frantically. "I can't go back to my room. If he finds out his notebook is missing, he's going to know I took it. You have to help me. Please. I don't want to die."

Officer Darling picks up her phone. "I need you to come escort a student to student housing for a new room assignment immediately." She pauses. "I'll be calling his roommate into the station now." She hangs up. "Paul, Officer Casey will be arriving shortly to work out a new room assignment for you. Even if this turns out to be something else, I don't think you and Mr. Michaelson should room together any longer."

"Thank you, but what about my stuff? I'll need to pack."

"Officer Casey will accompany you to do that as well. We'll make sure Mr. Michaelson is not present while you're moving your things out of the room."

"Are you going to arrest him?" Paul asks.

"I'm calling him in for questioning. I'm afraid we'll need more evidence before we can definitively say he's responsible for Professor Monaghan's murder."

Paul looks at me. "I'm scared. If he's not arrested, he can find me in my new room or on campus. I'm not going to be safe here anymore." He breaks down and sobs into his hands.

"I think we need to contact his parents," I suggest.

Officer Darling nods. "Of course. We'll see to that, too." She stands up. "Now, seeing as you two are not police officers and do not have any reason to be on campus, I'm going to have to insist you both leave and allow us to handle the matter from here."

We gave them what might be a key piece of evidence, and they're kicking us off campus? It's not exactly the thank you I was expecting.

"My brother is a police detective with the Swan Creek Police Department," Nolan says, and I'm a reporter, so I think asking us to leave is a bit unnecessary.

"Have your employer call me to confirm you're covering this story, and then we'll talk. As for your brother, he is welcome to come to campus and speak with us." Her gaze is penetrating. She's not going to budge on this.

"Come on, Nolan," I say. I place my hand on Paul's shoulder, and he looks up at me. "It's going to be all right. The campus police won't let anything happen to you, and I'm sure your parents will come as soon as they're contacted. You did the right thing, Paul."

He nods.

Nolan and I walk out of the building, and I notice another officer follow us out. I guess Officer Darling didn't trust us to leave on our own after we stayed the first time she thought we were going. I can't blame her there.

We walk back to Nolan's car and get in. "Well, I guess it's over."

"I guess so. I'll be happy when I hear about it on the news."

Nolan drives me back to my office so I can get my car. "Any chance you want to go to dinner to celebrate?" he asks me.

It's getting late, and I don't have much of an appetite. "Not tonight. I just want to go home and crawl into bed."

"Okay, good night, Sydney."

"Good night." I get into my car and drive the nine miles home. When I pull into the driveway, a patrol car immediately blocks me in. "What now?" I say as I get out and face Detective Lange.

"I hear you and my brother took a road trip."

"What about it? Are you here to thank us for doing your job?"

"No. I'm here to warn you, on the off chance you didn't actually kill Malcolm Monaghan."

"Of course, I didn't. Emmett Michaelson did."

"Maybe. I guess we'll see, which is why I'm here to tell you that I was contacted by campus police. They filled me in and told me when they tried to get a hold of Emmett, he ran."

"What do you mean he ran? Where?"

"They think he might be on his way here."

"For what reason?"

"To find the two people who came to campus and accused him of murder."

Chapter Sixteen

I'm honestly not sure which is worse: being accused of murder or being put in witness protection in Detective Lange's house. After he picked me up last night, he grabbed Nolan as well. I slept in his guest room, while Nolan took the couch. I stayed in the room all night, not wanting to talk to anyone. Nolan gave up trying after his third attempt. It's not that I'm upset with him. I'm upset with the situation. According to Detective Lange, I can't go to work or leave this house until Emmett Michaelson is found. I'm officially on lockdown, and I'm not permitted to tell anyone why, which is going to be awful for my practice.

I dial Lena's number first thing in the morning. "Lena, it's Sydney. I woke up with a fever this morning. I'm going to have to cancel my appointments today and possibly tomorrow." Maybe longer. I have no idea how long it will take the police to find Emmett.

"Oh no. I heard another wave of the flu was going around. Do you think that's what it is?"

"It might be. I'll keep you posted."

"Well, I'll handle canceling your appointments. You get plenty of rest and drink lots of fluids."

"Thanks, Lena. I appreciate it." I end the call and let out a deep breath when someone knocks on the door.

"Nolan, I'm not in the mood to talk," I say from the bed.

"It's Annabelle," comes the voice on the other side of the door.

I get up and open the door. "Good morning," I say.

Drew's wife holds out a cup of coffee to me. "I thought you could probably use this."

I take the mug. "Thank you. That was very thoughtful of you."

"I'm sorry you're wrapped up in all of this. I told Drew there's no way you killed that man. I said it right from the start. I mean why would you kill someone you've never even met? It didn't make any sense."

"Well, I guess finding the body and owning the same kind of wine that poisoned Malcolm made me look guilty in his eyes."

She smiles and shakes her head. "He wrongfully accused you of murder, and you're defending him?"

"Not really. It's sort of my job to see things from other people's perspectives and understand their motivation."

"Yeah, well, that's supposed to be Drew's job as well, but he's not the best at it." She laces her hands in front of her. "I mean, look at his relationship with Nolan. That's his brother, yet Drew can't see that the problems between them are all because he resents not being an only child."

Oh, boy. Does she want me to repair the relationship between Drew and Nolan?

"I'm thankful we don't have children because how would I even begin to explain why they can't see their uncle?"

"Did Drew not want to have kids because he feared sibling rivalry?" I ask.

Annabelle nods. "My father and mother were both twins. Drew was worried we'd have twins if I got pregnant. It was a big source of tension in our marriage for years. But then I got caught up in my career and realized I'd have to give it all up if I did have kids. We're talking about possibly fostering a child in a few years, though. An older child who needs a place to live until they turn eighteen."

"That's nice," I say, mostly because I don't want to have this conversation with her.

"Well, anyway, I have to get going to work. I just wanted to let you know I made eggs, toast, and bacon. They're in the kitchen if you're hungry. But if you do want some, I'd hurry. Nolan is already digging in." She must not know Nolan well at all. I wonder if he was even invited to their wedding.

"Thanks again." I raise the mug and shut the door after she walks down the hall. I wait a few minutes after I watch her car pull out of the driveway before I leave the room.

Nolan looks up from his newspaper when I enter the kitchen.

"I didn't know they still made physical newspapers," I joke.

"Ha-ha," he says. "Are you still angry with me?"

"Why would I be angry with you?" I ask, placing my mug on the table and grabbing a plate on the counter that I'm assuming Annabelle left out for me. I scoop some eggs from the pan and grab two slices of bacon before returning to the table.

"You didn't want to talk to me last night."

"I didn't want to talk to anyone. I needed time to process everything."

"I thought you were upset that I brought Drew into this and now you're being forced to stay at his house until Emmett Michaelson is found."

I sit down and fork a bite of eggs. "Oh, I'm definitely not happy about any of that, but it's not your fault. Even if you didn't tell campus police that Drew was your brother, they would have contacted him about Emmett anyway. Drew is the lead detective on Malcolm's murder."

"I suppose you're right. Still, I'm glad you don't blame me."

"How are you holding up under the circumstances?" I ask him.

He sips his coffee before answering. "Well, let's see. I finally got to meet my sister-in-law."

I was right. Nolan wasn't invited to the wedding. "I'm sorry."

He shrugs. "It is what it is. I can't change Drew. Annabelle seems nice, though."

"She does. I was surprised when she apologized to me for the way Detect—Drew treated me."

Nolan gives a short, forced laugh. "I guess she's used to apologizing for his behavior, too."

"It seems to be a common trend for the people in his life."

"She and I would probably have a lot to talk about. Maybe that's why he hasn't let me near her before."

"Have you considered why he's doing so now?" I ask.

"What do you mean? I'm assuming he was directed to by the chief of police."

I shake my head. "I doubt that. Why keep us here with no one watching us?"

"Oh, we're being watched. There was a patrol car here this morning before Drew left."

"But my point is, they could have held us at the station or at a safe house. Instead, Drew brought us to his home."

"What, do you think this is his weird way of inviting me into his life?"

It's my turn to shrug. "I won't pretend to know him well enough to guess his motivation, but I think it means something."

"The only thing I can think of is he's testing me to see if I'll actually stay put and do what he says."

Nolan is viewing this as Drew's way of seeing if he's worth letting him into his life after all this time. "He's being pretty trusting leaving us here while he keeps investigating."

"Well, he can't trust me that much if there's an officer stationed outside."

I bob one shoulder. "A single officer can't be that hard to slip past, especially when there are two of us to figure out a way to do it."

He laughs. "I can't figure out which one of us is the bad influence on the other."

"It might be a toss-up," I say.

"What's your plan?" He forks another bite of his breakfast.

"We need to find Emmett."

"You don't think him running is an admission of guilt?"

"Oh, it most likely is. I just don't trust your brother to catch Emmett and put an end to all of this."

Nolan smiles. "I can't say I blame you." He sips his coffee before saying, "I'm sorry you have to cancel all your sessions with your patients."

I'm really only worried about one of them. My others have been doing really well. Of course, I can offer to do phone sessions for anyone who really needs to talk to me today. "It's not your fault. If anything, I'm the one who's sorry. You didn't have to get wrapped up in any of this." It was my date gone wrong. Nolan shouldn't have to be in protective custody right now. He only is because he decided to connect with me.

"I made that decision, and given the chance to do it all over again, I wouldn't change a thing." He reaches across the table and squeezes my hand.

I'm still amazed at how comfortable it is to be around him. I could understand if we were good friends growing up and reconnected all these years later. But I never knew him as more than someone I went to school with.

"You're dying to bust out of here, aren't you?" he asks.

It was one thing to give in to Detective Lange's plan when it saved me from having to sleep alone in my apartment where Emmett Michaelson could have hunted me down and killed me without anyone knowing. But now that it's daylight, my courage has returned.

"I'd love to shower and get a clean change of clothes."

"Want to bust out of here?" he asks me.

"Are you offering to help me escape, or are you planning to free yourself as well?"

"Depends. Is that an invitation to go with you?"

I cock my head at him, trying to figure him out. How is it possible that he's changed so much since high school?

"Sorry." He looks down at his plate. "I'm not usually this forward. I think seeing you now has made me so mad at my teenage self. We could've been…" He meets my gaze. "We could have been so much more if I wasn't so afraid to talk to you. But here I am now, being overly forward to try to make up for it, and honestly, I'm not sure that's much better. Or any better for that matter."

"I think you're doing fine. I like honesty." Malcolm and I never would have worked out even if our date had turned out differently, because the moment I found out he'd been seeing his ex-wife, I would have removed myself from the equation. I don't think he was capable of being honest with himself about his feelings, so there's no way he would have been honest with me.

"I've been told I'm too blunt at times."

"I find that oddly refreshing."

He smiles. "Okay, then let's make a plan to bust out of here." He stands up and brings his empty breakfast plate to the sink, where he rinses it off before loading it into the dishwasher.

I finish my coffee, and a plan begins to form in my mind. "I bet the officer out there would love some coffee."

Nolan turns to me and squints as he leans back against the counter. "I'm not sure I understand what you're getting at."

"I think it would be nice to offer him an extra large coffee. After all, he is working hard to protect us right now. Offering him something to drink is the least we could do." I smirk.

"Okay, I know you're up to something, but I still can't figure it out."

I stand up and walk over to the coffee pot, inspecting how much is left. I open the cabinet above the counter and find a large coffee mug. I pour the contents of the pot into the mug. "There's one downside to drinking coffee. You can't drink all that much before you need to use the bathroom."

Nolan starts laughing. "Your plan is to give him so much coffee he needs to come in here and use the bathroom?"

"Do you have a better idea?" I ask. "Once he's in the bathroom, you and I can make a run for it."

"Your plan is crazy enough that it might actually work. Let's do it."

I open the refrigerator and find more coffee grinds. Just in case the officer stationed outside needs to drink several cups before having to use the bathroom, I brew another pot. Once I have that set up, I turn to Nolan with a coffee mug in my hand. "Time to go introduce ourselves to the officer who's protecting us."

He smiles and follows me out of the house.

We only make it a few steps outside before the officer gets out of his car and approaches us, his hand on the gun holstered at his hip. "What's wrong?" he asks.

"Nothing is wrong," I say. "We thought you might need a little caffeine boost."

The officer looks up and down the road, making sure there's no threat to us at the moment. Once he's satisfied, he reaches for the cup I'm holding out to him. "Thank you. That was very thoughtful of you both."

"Do you have to stay stationed out here the entire time, or are you allowed to come inside the house?" I ask.

"I'm supposed to stay out here."

"Well, if you need anything, let us know. Detective Lange's wife made us a nice spread for breakfast. There's also plenty of coffee left. We'd be happy to share."

The officer smiles at us. "I'm Officer Cardell by the way."

"Nice to meet you," I say. "I'm assuming you already know who we are."

He bobs his head and sips his coffee. "Thank you again for thinking of me. I should really get back in my car now."

Nolan and I turn around and head back inside the house. I'm not the most patient person, so sitting here waiting for Officer Cardell to need to use the bathroom feels like it takes forever. After about twenty minutes, I carry a pot of coffee outside to refill Officer Cardell's mug. I spend the next half hour pacing the floor in the kitchen. I'm about to bring him another refill for his coffee when there's a knock at the front door.

Nolan and I exchange a look. Then he answers the front door.

Officer Cardell smiles at us, but he looks uncomfortable. "Would you mind if I use the restroom for a moment?"

"Not at all." Nolan steps aside to let him into the house. "I'll show you where it is. Follow me."

While he brings Officer Cardell to the bathroom, I hurry into the room where I slept last night and grab my purse. I want to be ready to leave the second Nolan gives the all clear. As I walk by the bathroom in the hallway, I pretend to be searching for something in my purse just in case Officer Cardell sees me. But as I pass the bathroom, I see the door's already shut.

Nolan is waiting for me in the living room. Without saying a word, we hurry outside. Since neither one of us has a vehicle here, we're forced to walk. We cut through the neighbor's yard to avoid being seen on the road. Two houses down from Drew Lange's, there is a fenced-in backyard. Nolan gives me a boost over the fence and then follows me into the backyard. We crouch down and watch through the fence to see what Officer Cardell will do when he realizes we're gone.

It takes a few minutes, but Officer Cardell comes running outside. He looks around frantically in every direction and then pulls out his phone. I can't hear what he saying from this faraway, but I'm sure he called Detective Lange to tell him we ran. We watch as Officer Cardell gets his directive. To my surprise, he doesn't get into his car and leave. I thought he would be searching the neighborhood for us, knowing we would be traveling on foot. But it seems like Detective Lange told him to stay put. He must be sending out another officer to patrol the neighborhood for us. I can only imagine how angry he is right now. This isn't going to do anything to repair the relationship between Drew and Nolan, but I can't really worry about that at the moment.

Nolan and I cross the backyard and head for the woods.

"I'm starting to think we should've planned this through a little more," Nolan says as we walk aimlessly through the woods. "I'm not even sure where we are."

To be honest neither am I, but I don't see how mentioning that will help our situation any. So I keep walking as if I know where I'm going. "I think if we keep heading in this direction, we should wind up at the back entrance to the park." As soon as I say it out loud, I start laughing.

"What is so funny?" Nolan is looking at me like I have three heads.

"I just realized that the proximity of Drew's house to the park would give him the perfect opportunity to have killed Malcolm."

Nolan quirks an eyebrow at me. "You don't really think Drew had anything to do with the murder, do you?"

"Are you questioning if I think your brother tried to frame me for murder?"

He bobs one shoulder. "It's not as crazy as it sounds."

It takes us a few minutes, but we make it to the park. Where we emerge from the road is not by the willow tree. But my theory that the killer used the woods to leave the park still holds strong. "I think we should check out the woods behind the willow tree," I say.

"Are you trying to recreate the steps the killer might have taken?"

"It makes sense, doesn't it?"

"It does, but I'm sure the police have already swept the area for footprints."

Since there is no snow on the ground, and it hasn't rained for days, I doubt any footprints would be on the ground. Even though it's been a pretty mild winter, the ground is still too cold for an average person to leave imprints when they walk. But that doesn't mean there isn't other evidence for us to find.

"You must think my brother is the worst police detective in the world," Nolan says.

"Worst might be a bit of an exaggeration. I'm not one for extremes."

We walk over to the willow tree, which is marked off with police tape. I head straight for the woods behind the tree. Plenty of people use the path that winds around the park, but not many go into the woods themselves.

"What exactly are we looking for?" Nolan asks.

I'm tempted to say a vial of poison, but I know I'm not that lucky. We search for over an hour and find nothing.

"I think it's time we give up," Nolan says.

I hate to admit it, but he's right. Whoever killed Malcolm covered their tracks a little too well. And now that I ran from Detective Lange's protective custody, I'm going to look even guiltier in his mind.

Chapter Seventeen

I was convinced Detective Lange did not do a proper search of the area because he was so certain I was the murderer. Now I've allowed that to cloud my judgment to the point where I made myself look guilty. I should have stayed at Detective Lange's house until Emmett was found.

"I think we've made a big mistake," I say.

"Do you think we're looking in the wrong place for evidence?"

"No, that's not it. What if Emmett Michaelson ran knowing it would force us into protective custody? We might be doing exactly what he wanted us to do."

"Sydney, there's no way Emmett could have known we would run from the police, so if you think he set us up, you're reaching."

"We don't know anything about Emmett, but if he did try to frame me, he probably followed me like he followed Malcolm. He could have studied me to see how I would react in different situations."

"You're thinking too much like a psychologist. Emmett is a college student, one who needs a baseball scholarship to even attend the school. He wouldn't be able to come up with a plan like this."

I need some time alone to clear my mind. "I want to go home. I need to shower and change."

"You know that is the first place Drew will go to look for you. It's too risky."

"I'll go to my office then. I always keep a change of clothes there."

"And Drew knows exactly where your office is as well."

"Then what do you suggest?"

"Let's go back to the college. I can't see Emmett throwing away his baseball scholarship over all of this, especially if he did kill Malcolm to keep the scholarship."

I stop searching the ground and kick an acorn. "You can't possibly think he's hiding out at the college somewhere."

"Where else would he go?"

"The police are going to be all over that campus. Emmett's own roommate believes he committed murder."

"Think, Sydney. You're the psychologist."

"A second ago you told me I was thinking too much like a psychologist. Now you want me to think like one?"

"We need to figure out where Emmett would go to hide."

I lean against the trunk of a tall tree. The only thing Emmett has going for him is baseball. Nolan is right to assume Emmett wouldn't just walk away from that. But I'm sure the police are keeping a close eye on both the dorm and the locker room. I also don't think Emmett would be stupid enough to go back home since campus security already has his home address.

He'd need basic necessities. Shelter and food. He could have checked into a hotel for the night or slept in his car, if he has one on campus. Of course, using his own car is risky since the college would have that on file as well since he'd need a permit to park the car on campus. Every direction I go in turns out to be a dead end.

"Maybe one of his teammates is hiding him," Nolan suggests.

"I'm sure campus police is interviewing all of them."

Nolan huffs. "I never realized how awful Drew's job is. There are so many questions and no answers."

There are answers. We just haven't come up with them yet.

My first instinct was to go home, even though I know Detective Lange could find me there. People are always drawn to sources of comfort when they're scared. It's only natural, so what if Emmett did try to at least contact his parents? Not that his parents would hand him over to the police. They might even lie and say he never contacted them. They aren't a source I'm willing to trust.

"He likes notes," I say, thinking aloud.

"Yeah, so?"

"If Malcolm didn't bring that wine last Friday, why was he drinking it?"

"Maybe Emmett left it under the tree, and Malcolm thought you put it there."

"Then there would be a note," I say. "Emmett could have left a note pretending it was from me and saying I'd be back in a few minutes because I left something in my car."

Nolan snaps his fingers. "Right. So Malcolm pours a glass and starts drinking."

"But he only poured one glass."

"Not a very thoughtful guy forgetting to pour you some and then starting without you."

"Unless the note told him to do exactly that," I say, not sure if that's what I believe happened or if I'm trying to defend my date to make myself feel better about getting involved with a man who was clearly keeping a lot of secrets.

"It would make more sense that Malcolm brought the wine himself. You never mentioned that particular wine in a conversation you two had?" he asks.

"No, why?"

"Well, I thought that might explain why he happened to have the same bottle Drew found in your basement."

The truth is, Malcolm and I seemed to have a lot in common. That's why I agreed to meet him and why I talked to him and not anyone else on the dating app. It was uncanny how similar we were as far as our tastes went. As kids, we both hated melted cheese but loved shredded or sliced cheese cold. We both gave up eating meat during college for no apparent reason at all and began eating it again after graduation. It's surreal, but every time I told Malcolm something about me, he had a similar story. "What if he was lying to me?" I say aloud.

"Who? About what?"

"Malcolm. What if all the things he agreed with me on weren't real?"

"He was a psychology professor like he said. And Gerard Cowen was after Malcolm's teaching schedule, too."

"I can't help suddenly questioning everything. I mean what are the odds our lives were that parallel to each other?"

"They weren't," Nolan says. "You were in the same field, but your professions were different. And he was married before. You've never been married, right?"

"No, I haven't."

He steps toward me and grabs me by my shoulders so he can peer into my eyes. "Then don't do this to yourself. Even if Malcolm did lie about most things, that's on him, not you."

He's right. It's exactly what I'd tell a patient of mine in a similar situation. "Thank you. I needed to hear that."

"Any time. Now, what do we do?"

"Right now, we have to realize that we're officially running from the police just like Emmett Michaelson is. That means we can't go near the college because campus police might see us and arrest us on the spot."

"You think Drew called them." He considers if for a second and then bobs his head. "You're probably right. He's going to have all hands on deck looking for us as well as Emmett."

My phone rings in my pocket. I pull it out to see it's Autumn.

Nolan covers my phone with his hand. "Don't answer that. Drew might be with her and using her to find us."

"Autumn would never go along with that. She's my best friend, and she'd get herself put in handcuffs before she ever gave up my location to Detective Lange."

"You're positive?" Nolan asks.

"One hundred and fifty percent," I say, looking him in the eye. I trust Autumn with my life.

He nods and lowers his hand.

"Syd, where on earth are you? Drew Lange was just here to see if I've seen you."

"I can't tell you where I am. If I do, you'd lie for me, and I don't want that. I'm safe. That's all that matters."

"Well, he's already been here, so why don't you come hide out in my office?"

"No. I'm not letting you get involved in this, Autumn."

"I already am. I've helped you interview people, and I was questioned by the police. I'm not about to turn my back on my best friend. I don't care how dangerous this is."

I hate to play this card, but it's the only way I'm going to get her to listen to reason. "Autumn, I love you, and I appreciate you wanting to help, but think about the youth center. If you get arrested for aiding and abetting a murder suspect, you could lose everything you and Aaron worked so hard to build there. Those kids need you more than I do right now. You have to think of them."

She exhales loudly. "You're right, but I hate this. There has to be something I can do."

"If Detective Lange questions you again, tell him you spoke to me and I told you I ran to try to draw out Emmett Michaelson. Can you do that?"

"Of course, I can. I'll do better. I'll call Detective Lange and tell him exactly that right now. Maybe it will make him focus on finding Emmett instead of you guys."

"Thanks, Autumn."

"Be safe, and stay with Nolan."

I look at Nolan and nod. "I will." I end the call and pocket my phone. "She's going to call your brother and tell him we're trying to draw Emmett out of hiding."

"That won't stop Drew. He'll use Autumn's phone to try to trace where you called from."

"Can he do that?" I ask.

Nolan nods. "Don't ask me for all the specifics on how it's done, but I've seen the police do exactly that on other stories I've covered."

I think about calling Autumn back and telling her to abort the plan, but I stop myself. "Let's let her do it. We'll leave the park now before the police show up." If the police trace the call here, they'll surely think I've returned to the scene of the crime. And the fact that Nolan is with me might make them suspect he was my accomplice all along.

"Then we need to move. Right now."

He's right. We need to get as far away from the park as possible.

We take off through the woods again, not heading back toward Detective Lange's house but going around the park instead. We come out on a road I don't recognize at first.

"Where are we?" Nolan asks, out of breath.

We could both use showers after our impromptu morning jog.

I look around. "Let's go that way." I point to my left. "I think that might bring us to the main road. This sort of looks like the back road that goes to the housing development where Malcolm lived."

Nolan nods and follows me. I'm grateful it's too cold for snakes because we're running through woods and overgrown empty lots to avoid being on the road where a patrol car could easily spot us. My pulse races every time I hear a car coming our way, but none is a patrol car. I'm assuming only people who live in the residential community use this road. I realize my fear of all snakes is irrational, and as a psychologist, I should be able to overcome my fear. Believe me I've tried. I've forced myself to look at pictures of them until seeing them on a television screen or in a magazine didn't bother me anymore. And I even made myself pet one once at a zoo, but when I see them in the wild, I still scream my head off and try to jump into the arms of the closest human to me. So, I guess I'm a work-in-progress.

"Hey, we can go into the gym to shower and get cleaned up," Nolan says once we reach the main road.

"I don't have a gym membership," I say.

"I do, and I'm allowed to bring a guest on a day pass."

It's a public place, though. If the police released our photographs to the press, we might be plastered on every TV and smartphone within a hundred miles. "Too risky. Your brother might have the entire town searching for us by now."

Nolan pulls out his phone. "I doubt it. That would be like Drew admitting he can't handle this on his own. He's already going to look stupid for letting us get away. We were in his home after all."

I didn't look at it that way. Detective Lange has a big ego, and I doubt he'll let us bruise it.

Nolan shakes his head after scrolling through his phone. "Nothing about us in the local news. My boss would have called me anyway to see if I was undercover on a story before I officially start work."

"All right. I guess we hit the gym."

"We can buy new clothes from the shop in there, too. I don't know about you, but mine don't smell so fresh anymore." He pulls his jacket and shirt away from his chest and wrinkles his nose. "This isn't the impression I wanted to make on you."

"You know what would make a great impression on me?" I ask.

"What?"

"Solving this case so I don't get arrested."

He smiles and nudges me toward the gym. "I'm on it."

We walk inside, and the girl at the desk gives us a strange look. "Why do you two look like you've already worked out?"

"We ran here," he says. "It's a good warmup before hitting the weights."

She shrugs. "Suit yourselves."

I walk over to a rack of sweatshirts and sweatpants. Not exactly my style, but I grab a lavender crewneck sweatshirt with the gym's logo on the front. I'm about to grab matching sweatpants when I spot a rack of yoga pants. At least that's a little better. I never understood the appeal of sweatpants. They've always made me feel like I was wearing my dad's clothes. I grab a pair of yoga pants instead. When I turn around, Nolan is already at the register with some sweats and a hoodie.

"Throw yours up here," he tells me.

"No way. You're not paying for all of this stuff."

"You can pay me back later. Come on."

I put my sweatshirt and pants on the counter. The girl finishes ringing up the sale, and Nolan hands her some cash. I'm assuming he's not using a credit card to avoid Drew tracing it to locate him. Smart, although it makes me feel even more like a criminal.

After getting my guest pass, I follow Nolan down the stairs. "The women's locker room is right over there. They have complimentary shampoo and stuff in the men's room, so I'm assuming the women's locker room is stocked, too. I'll meet you back here in a few minutes."

I nod and walk into the locker room. There are only a few women inside. I smile at them in greeting and head for the showers. Like Nolan said, there's a basket on the counter where the row of sinks are, and inside the basket is an assortment of individual trial size bottles of shampoo and conditioner along with tiny bars of soap no longer than my thumb. I grab one of each and go to the first available shower.

I clean off quickly, forgetting I don't have a towel to dry myself. I groan and use the sweater I was wearing as a makeshift towel. Another woman sees me and approaches with a hand towel.

"Here. It's not big, but it beats using your sweater."

I'm slightly embarrassed that I'm naked in front of this woman, but she seems used to this. Most of me is covered by the tiny curtain in front of the shower stall, but I'm sure she's getting an eyeful of me. "Thanks." I take the towel and do my best to tug the curtain so it's covering more of me. I get dressed quickly and step out. I expect to see the woman who gave me the towel, but she's gone. Not sure what to do with the towel since it isn't mine, I fold it and leave it on the bench directly outside of my shower stall. Then I walk into the area where the lockers are.

"Hey," comes a male voice, making me whirl around.

"Nolan, you can't come inside the women's locker room."

But it's not Nolan who steps out from behind the row of lockers. It's Emmett Michaelson.

"How did you find me here?" I ask.

"I followed you. I've been following you since you left campus yesterday."

Of course, he did. His roommate warned us he was stalking Malcolm. Emmett had a notebook detailing his stalking. What made me think he wouldn't follow us?

No. I know what happened. I considered the choices a person accused of a crime would have. I just failed to think of the other option. The one Emmett actually chose: to confront his accuser. He came directly to me.

Chapter Eighteen

I backpedal toward the exit, keeping an eye on Emmett since I have no idea what he plans to do to me.

He holds up one hand. "I'm not going to hurt you. I want to explain what happened."

Explain? "I think I've already figured out what happened. You were angry with Malcolm for jeopardizing your scholarship. You knew about my date with him, and you used that to kill him and make me look like the guilty party."

"No. I didn't know about you. I only heard Professor Monaghan talking about his date. He didn't mention you by name at all."

"Then you didn't break into my house and steal a bottle of wine from my basement?"

"No. I don't even know where you live." He shrugs. "Like I said, I started following you from the campus, and you've only gone to that cop's house, the park, and here. You haven't been home."

"You know where Professor Monaghan lived, though. You went to his house on more than one occasion."

"I did. I won't deny that. I didn't handle any of it well, but I swear I didn't kill him. You have to believe me." His tone is full of desperation.

"Why are you pleading your case to me instead of the police?" I ask.

"Because you seem to know more than they do."

He has a point there.

"And besides, the police are looking for me now. If I go to the station, they're going to arrest me."

"Running from them wasn't your best idea." Not that he's had a lot of good ideas from what I've seen.

"I know. It was stupid, but I panicked. You're not really Paul's aunt, right? You lied because you took my notebook and wanted to get out of my room before I figured it out."

"That's right. Why were you stalking Malcolm?"

"I had to change his mind about my grade. I'm not a slacker. I didn't fail because I didn't do the work. I'm just not smart. Baseball is all I have. If I lose my scholarship, I lose everything. I had to make him understand that. I mean, he has a degree in psychology. Shouldn't he have been able to figure that out? I even offered to do extra work, but he wouldn't let me."

I really don't know what to make of Malcolm. If Emmett really did plead for his grade nicely at first and Malcolm dismissed any chance of improving his standing in the class, maybe he isn't the compassionate man I thought he was. Maybe he fooled me about everything.

"You know he was messing around with his ex-wife, right?" Emmett asks me. "I saw it with my own eyes. You're lucky you never got to have that date with him. He wasn't a good guy."

"How did you find out about his ex-wife?" I ask.

Emmett avoids my eyes. "You know I was following him. When he wouldn't listen to reason, I took pictures of him with his ex. They went to lunch together all the time. At the campus, he pretended he didn't like her and that she'd show up unannounced, but that was an act. When it was just the two of them, they looked like a happy couple."

"His ex-wife is living with another man," I say.

"I know. I threatened to tell that guy. I thought Professor Monaghan would listen to me if I had something on him."

"You tried blackmailing him?"

"I'm not proud of it, but the guy was a total sleaze, so I didn't feel all that bad. I mean, think of the man Monaghan's ex-wife is cheating on. He had a right to know."

Jared wasn't exactly innocent either. "He was the man that broke up their marriage. Sherry Monaghan is living with the very same man she cheated on Malcolm with."

Emmett jerks his head back. "Whoa! Really? That's... I don't even know what to call that. It's messed up."

He's telling me. I feel like an idiot for being so conned by Malcolm in the first place.

"Did you tell Sherry's boyfriend the truth?" I ask.

Emmett looks ashamed. "I wasn't planning to. I just wanted to get Professor Monaghan to let me improve my grade. But when he wouldn't... I found out who the guy was."

"You know his full name?" I ask. Sherry only called him by his first name.

"Jared Hendershot."

I'm not about to take my eyes off Emmett to jot the name into my notes app on my phone so I commit the name to memory. Emmett might not be a murderer, but he's still a little unhinged, and since he's on the run from the police, I'm not willing to bet he won't try to hold me hostage to get out of town. I need to keep him talking until I can be sure Nolan is standing outside the locker room door. "How did you contact him?"

"I left him a message."

Emmett and his notes. Why am I not surprised? "What kind of message?"

"A note in his mailbox at his office in Dover. I had to make sure Sherry wouldn't find it first."

"You gave up the only leverage you had on Malcolm?" I ask. "Why would you do that?"

"Because Professor Monaghan clearly wasn't going to budge on my grade. I figured if I couldn't blackmail him for a better grade, then I might as well make him suffer somehow."

"What if it led to Sherry and Jared splitting up and Malcolm going back to her?" His plan could have backfired and gotten Malcom and Sherry together again.

He shrugs. "I figured no man would walk away like that."

He's right. No man would. Malcolm divorced Sherry when he discovered the affair. Jared... "It's Jared. Jared killed Malcolm after he read your note."

Emmett shakes his head. "No. No way. He's still with Sherry. I don't think he ever even got my note. He wouldn't still be with her if he did. He would have left."

"Not if he eliminated his competition." I think back on my conversation with Sherry. She said Jared didn't want to live in the house she once shared with Malcolm. He wouldn't after learning Sherry was seeing Malcolm behind his back. He knew she was still in love with him, and he killed Malcolm to put an end to it.

"You really think he did it?" Emmett asks me.

"I do." It makes more sense than Emmett killing Malcolm over a grade. People do crazy things for love.

"You have to tell the cops so they'll leave me alone."

Even if I do tell Detective Lange my theory, I still don't have proof, and Emmett fled, making him look really guilty.

"Emmett, look me in the eyes. Tell me you had nothing to do with Malcolm's murder."

"I can't. You said it's my fault because I told that guy about the affair."

"Okay, but you didn't know Jared would kill Malcolm, right? That wasn't your intention?"

"No. I didn't want the guy dead. I hated him and thought he was—"

I hold up a hand to stop him. "You're trying to make a case for your innocence, so choose your words carefully."

"Right. No, I didn't know Jared would kill Malcolm."

"All right. I need you to get out of here."

"How?" he asks. "The police are looking for me. Where do I go?"

He's been doing well staying off their radar even though he's been following me. "Whatever you've been doing. It's working. There were two cops at Detective Lange's house, and neither knew you were watching the place."

"So I keep following you?" he asks.

"That's not exactly what I'm saying. Lay low. I'm going to find a way to prove Jared Hendershot killed Malcolm. Once I do, you can come forward and tell the police you ran because you were scared of being arrested for a crime you didn't commit."

"Do you think that will really work?" he asks.

"Honestly, I'm not sure. I mean, you did stalk Malcolm, and the police have your notebook proving that, but Malcolm is dead, so it's not like he can press charges."

"What if I go back to school in a few days, and if the police come looking for me, I'll say I took off because I needed to clear my head after thinking my scholarship was over?"

"I can't tell you what to do, Emmett. That's for you to decide."

"You're running from the police, too. How are you going to get out of that?"

"Hopefully by finding the real killer. That should help both of us."

"Good luck," he says. "I hope you catch him for both our sake."

The door to the locker room opens, and Emmett ducks behind the row of lockers again. I use the opportunity to slip out into the hallway where Nolan is waiting for me.

"I was about to ask someone to go in there and look for you," he says, stepping toward me so he can keep his voice down. "Is everything okay?"

"Emmett followed us. He's in there."

Nolan takes a step toward the women's locker room, but I grab his arm. "No, it's okay. He's not the killer. I think I know who is."

"We need to go somewhere private," he says, taking my hand in his and pulling me toward the back exit.

I look down at our hands, wondering why this feels so normal. He brings us down the hallway to a door. Then he uses his gym membership keycard to get us outside without setting off the alarm on the door. I'm not sure why they lock people inside like this, but I guess maybe it has to do with not allowing nonmembers to sneak in through this door. Nolan looks around the parking lot.

We really need a car. I know who the killer is, or at least I think I do, but he works in Dover, and there's no way we'll get there on foot.

A car pulls up to us, making us jump backward so we're up against the building. The driver lowers the window. "Get in."

It's Emmett.

Nolan looks at me, and I nod, fully aware that Emmett could be lying and this could be a trap. I don't see any other option at the moment, though. We both get in the back seat, wanting to stick together just in case.

"Is this your car?" I ask Emmett.

"Yeah. I know the cops are probably looking for it, so we'll have to take back roads."

Nolan and I were helping Emmett stay off the radar by taking back roads earlier when he was following us. I'm sure the police are assuming he'd take the fastest route out of town.

Emmett pulls out of the parking lot. "You two should slouch down back there. I don't live around here, so while the police are looking for my car, they might not recognize my face as easily as yours."

I don't bother to tell him they'll stop him based on the car alone. He's clearly scared, and since he's helping us, I don't want to do anything that might make him decide he should kick us out of the car.

"We need to get to Dover where Jared Hendershot works," I tell Emmett.

"I figured as much."

I fill Nolan in on what Emmett and I are theorizing happened last Friday night.

"Wait, that still doesn't explain the wine," Nolan says. "How would Jared know you even had it in your basement?"

"I don't have an answer to that question. We might need to wait for him to tell us that part."

"I doubt he's going to admit to murder," Emmett says. "Who in their right mind would?"

"Ah, but what murderer is in their right mind to begin with?" I ask.

"Good point."

"Emmett, you told me Malcolm wasn't really a good guy. Other than the affair with his ex-wife and not allowing you to pull up your grade by doing extra work, is there any other reason why you believe that's the case?"

"Yeah. He's a psychology professor, right?"

I nod, even though Emmett isn't looking in the rearview mirror and can't see me.

"Well, that means he should be able to figure out his students. You know, read their body language, interpret things they say, and get to know who really cares about their grades and who doesn't."

"I'm with you so far," I say.

"Okay, well, there's this girl in my class. She failed a test, yet somehow she has a B in the class."

"How do you know?" I ask.

"I heard her telling one of her friends. She said Professor Monaghan let her do extra credit."

"But he wouldn't do the same for you," I say.

"Exactly. Now consider this. How is it possible that he didn't know his wife was having an affair?"

He's right. Malcolm should have been able to pick up on the clues. Sherry's emotions are loud and clear. I'd never met her before, yet I knew exactly how she felt about Malcolm and why she was still living in their house. "You think Malcolm knew."

Emmett nods. "He didn't care because he was having an affair, too."

"With the girl in your class," I say. I suddenly feel sick. This guy lied to me over and over again, and I had no idea because I'd never met him in person. Lies are easily covered up in emails. And when we talked on the phone, the conversations were brief. He often said he had to go because a student entered his office. I thought he was dedicated to his work, but what if he was meeting with the girl in Emmett's class for "extra credit" as he called it. I swallow hard, angry with myself for being so easily fooled.

Nolan reaches for my hand on my lap and holds it between both of his. "This is not your fault. I'm sure he was good at fooling people. He could have used his psychology degree to help him do it."

"I still fell for it. I feel like such an idiot."

Emmett eyes me in the rearview mirror. "Lady, I don't know you, but I wouldn't take this personally. Some people are so good at lying they fool themselves, too."

I'm quiet for the rest of the ride because I spend the time considering I really am terrible when it comes to reading people in my personal life. Clients on my couch are no problem. But look at Nolan. I had no idea he liked me when we were growing up. And then there's Malcolm. I can't help wondering if this was all a game to him. Were Sherry, the girl in his class, and I all part of some sick experiment he was conducting to see how many women he could con at once? Was he trying to make a statement about the female population as a whole? Whatever it was, I hate that I was part of it. I'm also convinced Malcolm divorced Sherry to make himself seem more available to younger women.

Emmett pulls up to the building with no sign on the front at all. And even though the building is a decent size, there aren't many cars parked in the lot.

"Are you sure this is the lab where Jared works?" I ask, undoing my seat belt.

"I may not be smart, but I'm good at finding things. This is it."

"You might have a future as a private investigator," I say. His stalking skills and research abilities would be put to good use there.

Emmett turns around to face me. "A P.I." He smiles. "I kind of like the sound of that."

We get out of the car and start for the front door. When we walk inside, there's no receptionist or anyone around. I'm assuming this isn't a place that's visited by the public. The only people who come in here must be the chemists. It has to be a research facility more than anything else.

"How do we find him?" Nolan asks.

"We need to split up to cover more ground," I say.

"No way. I'm not leaving you." Nolan's expression couldn't be any sterner.

"Nolan, we can't go back home until we catch this guy."

He pulls his phone from his pocket. "I'm calling Drew. We can't make an arrest. We need him."

I didn't think that part through. "Okay, make the call."

The conversation isn't a fun one. I can hear Drew screaming on the other end. But Nolan tells him where we are and why. Then he tells Drew to get here as soon as possible. Drew gets in one sentence before Nolan hangs up on him.

"Okay, that's taken care of."

"Whoever finds Jared Hendershot calls the others with their location before confronting him so we can all talk to him together. Agreed?" I ask.

Emmett pulls out his phone and exchanges phone numbers with us. Then he points down the hallway to the left. "I'll head that way."

"Do you really think we can trust him?" Nolan asks me once Emmett is out of earshot.

He could have set us up. Brought us here as a trap. It's entirely possible that he and Jared Hendershot killed Malcolm together, and now Emmett brought us here to take care of us as well.

"Drew's on his way, right?"

Nolan nods. "I still think we should stick together in case this is a trap."

"All we're going to do is locate Jared. I don't plan to tackle him or anything like that. You were the football player, not me."

He smirks and squeezes my hand. "Be careful."

"Right back at ya," I say before turning down the hallway to our right. I look back once to see Nolan heading up the stairs in the center of the hallway.

I pass a few doors, none of them marked, so I press my ear to each and listen for sounds on the other side. I keep working down the hallway to the end where I come to a stairwell that only leads down. Knowing Jared made the basement at his house into an office, according to Sherry, I decide to go down.

I can hear noises before I approach the door at the end of the stairs. I peer through the small window in the door, but I can't see anything. I slowly open the door to see a giant room filled with all sorts of workstations. It looks like a high school lab room. At the far end is a man wearing goggles and pouring some sort of liquid into a beaker. He's turned away from me, so I duck into the room and hide behind a shelf.

I pull out my phone and dial Nolan. "I found him," I whisper into the phone as he picks up.

"Where?"

"Basement. He's doing some sort of experiment."

"Don't engage. Stay put, and don't let him see you. It's going to take Drew an hour to get here. He said he was calling the local police, but I don't know when they'll show up."

"I'll stay hidden. Don't worry." I end the call and pocket my phone as I keep an eye on Jared.

He walks around the lab table and disappears from view. I can't lose him, so I come out from behind the shelf and walk as silently as possible toward the lab station he was using, staying close to the side wall. The room is odd shaped, jutting out to the right up ahead, which is where Jared went.

I hear his voice. He must be making a voice recording about whatever experiment he's conducting down here. I stop at the end of a long metal shelf and carefully lean forward to get a glimpse around the corner. Something tugs on my jacket from behind, and then there's a loud clatter as a bin full of glass beakers falls to the cement floor and shatters everywhere.

"Who's here?" Jared yells, whirling around and coming face-to-face with me.

Chapter Nineteen

I debate making a run for it, but I still have the handle of the metal basket stuck to my jacket. I grab it and yank it free, holding it out in front of me as if it were a weapon. "Don't come near me."

He removes his goggles and tosses them onto the desk behind him. "How did you get down here?"

"The stairs," I say, thinking that's obvious.

"The door automatically locks when it closes." He's acting like he doesn't know who I am, but considering how much I've been fooled lately, I'm not willing to trust my ability to tell if he's being genuine right now or not.

I debate whether to confront him or wait for Nolan. Nolan was on the second floor, but it shouldn't take him long to get down here to the basement. Then what Jared said finally clicks. The door locks when it closes. It must not have fully closed when he came down here, but did it when I came into the basement? If so, Nolan won't be able to get to me.

"You're Jared Hendershot, right?" I ask, trying to buy myself time to think of a way out of here. I could make a run for it. The door locks from the inside, so I can still get out. As long as Jared can't outrun me. He looks physically fit, so I don't want to chance my only hope at escape yet.

"Who's asking?"

I still don't trust that he doesn't know who I am. He could be trying to lull me into a false sense of security. "I spoke to Sherry."

He cocks his head at me. "How do you know Sherry?"

"She told me you worked here."

"That doesn't answer my question. How do you know her?" He's getting visibly agitated. His nostrils flare, and his right hand is now in a fist.

"We had a mutual..." What do I even begin to call Malcolm? "Friend." I'm using the term very loosely.

"Who?"

"Malcolm Monaghan." I want to see his reaction to the name.

His chest rises and falls. "You knew Malcolm?"

"Not very well at all. Not as well as you seemed to think I did."

"What are you talking about?"

"You know where I live. You broke into my house and stole a bottle of wine from my basement."

"Lady, I don't even know who you are, let alone where you live. I didn't break into anyone's house."

His body language says he's telling the truth. Did Detective Lange lie about the wine rack? I never looked for myself. I didn't want any of my DNA in that basement at all so he couldn't prove I had been down there at some point. But that means I never saw the empty spot where he said a bottle was removed. He could have seen what he wanted to see as opposed to what was really there. Or Jared Hendershot is as skilled at lying as Malcolm was.

"You really don't know who I am?" I ask, wanting to read his body language and look for patterns that might indicate he's lying.

"Not a clue."

"I'm the woman Malcolm Monaghan had a date with last Friday night. I'm the one who found his body."

This time his face says so much. He knew all about the date at the park. That much I'm certain of. But something is throwing him off as well. "No. Malcolm was meeting…" He shakes his head. "It couldn't have been you."

The pieces of the puzzle click into place as I realize what really happened. "You thought he was meeting Sherry."

"The note. It said Sherry was seeing Malcolm behind my back."

So it was Emmett's note that set the murder plot into motion. "Yes, she was. Like you were seeing Sherry behind Malcolm's back while they were married," I say.

"How do you know about that?" he asks.

"Like I said, I was the one Malcolm was dating. Well, one of the women, I guess. I didn't know he was still seeing Sherry. He lied about a lot of things."

"They played us both then," he says, his tone changing as if he and I are suddenly comrades bonding over this common betrayal.

"Sherry had no idea you knew, then?" I ask.

"I never confronted her. Malcolm was egotistical. I figured he wanted to ruin our relationship to get back at us. That he was using her."

Malcolm used a lot of people. Does Jared think in some twisted way he was protecting Sherry by killing Malcolm? Is that what this was?

"And she has no idea you killed him."

"Why would she suspect me if she doesn't know I knew about the affair?"

She wouldn't. He thought his plan through. "How did you poison the wine?"

He gestures to his office. "Seriously? I'm a theoretical chemist."

"Theoretical," I repeat, but I realize how stupid it sounds considering we're standing in his lab where, moments ago, I caught him doing a very real experiment of some kind.

He smirks. "I see, so you think the word theoretical means I can't possibly know how to do actual experiments like a 'real' chemist." He makes air quotes around the word real.

"That's not what I'm saying." Does he realize he's completely confessed to murder? Why is he telling me all of this? Does he really think I'll be on his side and keep my mouth shut all because we were both being cheated on? I'm not even sure I consider it that since Malcolm and I weren't officially dating. We were never a couple.

"What are you saying then?" He steps toward me.

"I mean most people won't suspect you because your profession doesn't usually involve experiments, right?"

"Wrong. I conduct experiments all the time."

I still don't know how he got hold of the same wine Detective Lange found in my house. "So back to the wine, it wasn't the bottle from my basement?"

He shakes his head. "It was from *my* basement."

"Yours?" I thought his basement was a home office.

"Yeah, I guess Malcolm was a wine aficionado or whatever you call it. Sherry said that was the last bottle of his favorite wine. She said it cost a fortune, and when he realized he didn't take it in the divorce, it started a fight between them."

A fight they apparently moved past since he started seeing her again. But does that mean he thought the bottle was from Sherry and not me? Did he think it was a peace offering or something more? A Valentine maybe? I may never know the answer to that question because it's not like I can ask Malcolm myself. He's gone. And he took his true feelings about Sherry with him. For all I know, he started seeing her again to get that bottle of wine back. Maybe he was drinking it as a victory toast to his success.

"Why would you bring him the wine he loved?" I ask. "You must have hated him."

"Easy. I knew he'd drink it. He's been after that bottle since the divorce." That made it the perfect murder weapon. Jared knew how much Malcolm wanted it.

"But wouldn't you worry Sherry would suspect you when the bottle was found with Malcolm's body? She must have known it was the same one."

He shoves his hands into his pockets. "I guess it was a risk I was willing to take. I bet on him drinking enough to kill him before she showed up, and I was right."

"But you were wrong about who his date was with. Sherry didn't have plans with him that night."

"Yeah, well, now she won't ever have plans with him again, so it all worked out in the end."

Except for one loose end. Me. I have to make him think I'm relieved he killed Malcolm, or I'll never get out of here alive. "I guess I owe you a thanks. You saved me from winding up with a creep like Malcolm. Sherry and I both have you to thank for that."

"The cops think it's you, don't they? Because you found him. And now you're telling me you had the same kind of wine."

I can practically see him mentally working through a new plan. A plan to frame me, which I thought he was doing all along. "My bottle was still in my basement. That's why the police couldn't make any charges against me stick. In fact, I was in protective custody for a while." Maybe I shouldn't have said that. He might think I'm working with the police now to catch the real killer. I need to fix this and fast. "I talked to Sherry. She asked me to come here and warn you."

Jared narrows his eyes at me. "Uh-uh. A minute ago, you were surprised Sherry didn't figure out I killed Malcolm. Now you're trying to tell me she knows and sent you to warn me? That doesn't add up. You're lying through your teeth."

"No!" I hold up both hands and take a step back. "I know the guy who left you the note. We want to make sure you don't get caught, but neither of us wants to go down for this either."

Jared shakes his head. "Sorry, but someone has to be convicted for this murder, or the cops are going to keep digging around."

I take another step back. Nolan must be freaking out, trying to get into the locked basement. I need to get to that door.

"Where do you think you're going?" Jared lunges for me.

I scream and try to dodge the lab tables.

He grabs a hold of my jacket and yanks me backward. I fling my arms back, allowing me to slip out of the jacket all together as I run for the door.

"Stop!" he yells. He's fast, and he quickly closes the distance between us.

The next thing I know, I'm being tackled from behind. As I hit the floor, I see Nolan trying to break the glass in the door.

Jared pulls me to my feet and laughs. "Fireproof glass. Good luck getting through it."

"You can't get out," I say, and the police are on their way.

Jared pulls me closer to his body. "Then I guess I'm taking a hostage. You're going to get me safely out of this building, and then I'm going to kill you like I killed Malcolm."

Chapter Twenty

Jared brings me farther into the basement and starts rifling around on the shelves. I'm sure he's looking for a weapon. He can use my body as a human shield, but having me held by a weapon makes him even more intimidating. The police will have to listen to his demands.

"I'm so glad you came to see me today."

"My name is Dr. Sydney Warner," I say. Humanizing the victim is a ploy police use in hostage situations all the time, so I figure I should give it a try.

"Doctor?"

"I'm a psychologist."

He laughs. "And you were duped by Malcolm Monaghan and framed for murder? No offense, Doc, but I'm going to wager you're grossly overpaid and under skilled."

I grit my teeth to keep myself from lashing out at him. Let him think what he said is true. I need to get the upper hand, and playing dumb might not be a bad way to do it. "I guess that means you don't want to talk about your feelings," I say, still struggling under his grasp. The man must spend countless hours a week in the gym because he's much stronger than he looks.

"You want to try to psychoanalyze me, Doc?" He laughs and pulls a small blade from a metal box.

"What's with all the metal?" I ask.

"It's a lab. Explosions and fires can and do happen." He pulls me toward a window and peers out. "I guess you weren't lying about the police."

"Your plan isn't going to work."

He presses the blade to my cheek, and I wince. "If I were you, I'd hope it does."

"Why? You admitted you're going to kill me anyway. Why would I help you get out of here?"

He tugs me tighter to his chest. "I'm going to give you a choice. You can walk out of here with me and help me get to safety, or I'll open that door, let your boyfriend and the police inside, and then blow up this lab."

"You'd die in the process," I say.

"I'm confident you won't choose that option," he growls in my ear.

"What would Sherry want?" I ask him. "You did all of this so you two could be together without Malcolm getting in the way. Why would you throw it all away now?"

"What choice do I have? You brought the cops here. I can always come back for Sherry later."

"And do what? Kidnap her? Force her to be with you against her will?"

"Over time, she'll come to understand why I did it. That it was all for us. Because I love her."

"And what if she never does? Are you going to kill her, too? Could you look her in the eyes and take her life?"

"Stop it!" he snarls. "You don't know her."

"I know she still loved Malcolm. I know she wouldn't move out of that house or give up that bottle of wine because she was convinced Malcolm would come back to her. She regretted the affair with you. She was making amends for it."

"No!" He shoves me against the wall.

I hit my shoulder hard and go down.

He comes at me with the knife, and I kick my leg out, my foot connecting with his groin. He cries out and falls to his knees. I scramble to my feet. He makes one last ditch effort to swing the knife at me, but I run.

I rush to the door and pull it open. Nolan grabs me, and Detective Lange and several other police officers push their way past us into the basement, guns raised at Jared.

"It's okay," Nolan says. "It's over."

"He confessed."

"Shh." Nolan holds me to his chest.

Detective Lange walks back over to us. "How could you be so stupid? He was going to kill you."

They might not have heard Jared confess to killing Malcolm, but they witnessed him try to kill me through the small window in the door.

"I'm well aware, and you're welcome for solving your case. He confessed to murdering Malcolm. That bottle of wine was in Sherry's basement where Malcolm left it by accident in the divorce. He's wanted it back this entire time. Jared realized that made it the perfect murder weapon. He thought Malcolm was meeting Sherry that night at the park. Emmett Michaelson left Jared a note here at the lab, telling him about Sherry and Malcolm's affair. That's what caused Jared to plot Malcolm's murder. Emmett was only trying to make Malcolm pay for not letting him pull up his grade. He had no idea Jared would react that way.

Detective Lange stares at me in shock. "You figured all of that out?"

"What can I say? People will talk when they feel like the person they're talking to actually wants to listen."

Detective Lange clenches his jaw for a moment before saying, "You're both coming back to the station with me."

"Where's Emmett?" I ask.

"I haven't seen him," Nolan says.

I turn to Detective Lange. "He's a kid. Don't be too hard on him. He made some mistakes, but he's not a murderer. He feels awful that his note led to this, but there's no way he could have known it would. Don't ruin the kid's chance at a real future. I might have told him to focus his keen observational skills into a career as a private investigator. He seemed to like that idea."

Nolan smiles at me. "Giving more free therapy sessions I see."

"I owed him. I wouldn't have solved the case without his help," I say.

"Let's go. We have a long night ahead of us," Detective Lange says. "You two have a lot of questions to answer."

After Emmett sees the police bring Jared Hendershot out in handcuffs, he comes out of hiding and voluntarily returns to Swan Creek with us. He decides to help the police as much as he can, figuring that will help him in the long run. We all give our statements and answer a slew of questions from Detective Lange.

I'm exhausted by the time I finally crawl into bed, but I get the best night sleep I've had in almost a week.

Thursday morning, I go to the youth center. Autumn left me five voice mails, all asking for a full debriefing, as she called it, upon waking. I grab some breakfast at the diner first and run into Nolan as I'm paying my bill.

He slides into the seat across from me. "Is this seat taken?" he asks.

"It is now." I place my check and money at the edge of the table for the waitress. "Did you want to eat. I just finished, but I'll sit with you."

"No, I ate at home. I figured I might find you here."

"What made you think I wouldn't be at my office?" I ask when I notice how uncomfortable he looks.

"Okay, I went to your office first, and Lena told me you took the morning off and were having breakfast here."

"I moved my appointments to the afternoon. I have to go check in with Autumn so she can count my limbs and make sure I'm really okay after yesterday."

"Oh." His face falls.

"You want to tag along? I can introduce you to Aaron, Autumn's husband. He's a great guy. I think you two would get along."

"Why not? It's my last day off before I start my new job tomorrow."

"I guess that means I won't be seeing as much of you," I say.

"Oh, I don't know. The news business can be stressful. I might need to book a few sessions with you to help me unwind."

"Sorry, but I don't mix my personal life with my work life. If you were a patient of mine, I couldn't talk to you outside of my office."

"Well, I wouldn't want that," he says.

"Come on." I stand up, and he follows me out of the diner. We drive separately since we both have our cars.

The youth center doesn't have many kids in attendance today, and for some strange reason, Autumn and Aaron aren't here. Leslie, the woman who manages the place when they aren't around, comes over to us.

"Hey, Sydney. If you're looking for Autumn, she ran out in a hurry. Something about a house."

"She's on the hunt for a house," I tell Nolan. "She and Aaron are currently living in an apartment."

"You're welcome to stick around," Leslie says. "They left over two hours ago, so they should be back soon."

"Thanks, I will."

Leslie hurries off to the game room, where most of the kids are gathered.

"So, Autumn and Aaron run this place for kids who need a place to go?" Nolan asks me.

"Yeah. You know, kids whose parents work mostly, but they have classes here for homeschooled kids as well. That's who Leslie is with now. It gets them out of the house and socializing with other kids."

"That's great. Has the local paper done a story on this place yet?"

"No, and I've always wondered why they haven't. It's a great thing Autumn and Aaron are doing here."

"I agree. I'm going to talk to my editor about it tomorrow."

The door opens, and Autumn and Aaron walk in. "You might want to talk to Aaron about it first."

Autumn looks like she's about to explode, but I say, "Autumn, Aaron, this is Nolan Lange."

Aaron extends his hand.

"I was telling Sydney I'd love to write an article about this place and the work you two are doing here," Nolan says.

"Really?" Aaron's eyes light up. "I'd love that. Do you have a few minutes to talk now?"

"Good. You two talk." Autumn pulls me toward her office. "I bought Sherry Monaghan's house!" she shrieks.

"You did what?"

"I bought it. I called her this morning to offer my condolences after what happened with Jared, and I asked her what she was planning to do. She told me she couldn't stand to be here anymore. After all this, she wants a clean start. New house, new town. So I made an offer, and she accepted on the spot. We're closing in two weeks."

"I can't believe this."

"I know. I drove Aaron right over there to see the house again. He already knew which one it was, but I wanted him to see the inside. Sherry was just as happy as we are about this. I think she's relieved to be able to move on so quickly."

I'm sure Sherry feels guilty for both affairs. Whether Malcolm played her too to get his rare wine back or if his feelings were genuine, we'll never know. But I think Sherry's decision to move on is the right one. "This is fantastic news."

Autumn clasps her hands together, and her smile is so wide I'm afraid her face is going to split in two. "You know what this means, right? I'm one step closer to getting Aaron on board with the baby idea."

I hug her. "I'm happy for you, Autumn. And you're going to be living less than ten minutes from my place." I'd always envisioned her living in my neighborhood, but ten minutes is nothing. We'll make it work just fine.

"I know. Everything is falling into place. I'm thinking by the end of the year, the baby plan will be a go." She turns to look at Nolan. "Looks like it's your turn to get your life in order, starting with that man right there. He's absolutely gorgeous, and don't think I haven't noticed you two have been inseparable since you met up again."

"Easy, Autumn. I barely know Nolan. He's great, but I'm going to take this slowly." Of course, it feels like I've known him forever. He turns and smiles at me, and my stomach flutters.

"You're a goner," Autumn says. "Despite your protests, your true feelings are written all over your face. Let me know when we can all double date."

Double date. That's a safe way to get to know Nolan better. "Tomorrow," I say, and her eyes widen so much I'm worried they'll pop right out of their sockets.

"Are you serious?"

I nod. "I'm going to go ask him right now. I'll call you later with the details." I smile at her and walk over to Nolan and Aaron. "Can I steal him from you?" I ask Aaron.

"Be my guest," Aaron says.

"I'll be in touch about the article," Nolan tells him.

"I'm looking forward to it." Aaron waves to us.

I loop my arm through Nolan's, and we walk out of the youth center. He's held my hand a few times now, but this is the first occasion where I've initiated the contact.

"This is nice," he says, looking down at our linked arms.

"It is," I agree. "I wanted to say thank you for helping me with the case and sticking up for me where your brother was concerned."

He stops walking and faces me, leaning back against the driver's side door of his car. "Of course. I'm just glad you and I are finally connecting the way I always hoped we would."

"About that," I say.

His face falls, and I realize he thinks I want to talk because I'm going to tell him I only want to be friends. He thinks I'm trying to let him down easily. "Syd—"

"Would you have dinner with me tomorrow night?" I ask.

He looks like he's in shock.

"Not just me. Autumn and Aaron as well. I figured you could probably use some friends in town, and they're the best people I know."

"Oh. Friends. Yeah."

"Right. Aaron and Autumn would make great friends." I take a step toward him. "And I know it's a little late, but if you're looking for a Valentine, I think I might know someone to fit that bill, too." I lean forward and lightly press my lips to his.

At first, he doesn't move. Then his arms wrap around me, and he kisses me back.

"So, dinner? Is that a yes?" I ask when I pull away.

"It's a yes to all of it. Especially the last part." He laces his fingers through mine.

"Good because I think I got gipped out of the holiday this year."

"I think we can fix that, and at half the cost considering all the flowers and chocolate are on sale now that the actual day has passed."

"Make it dark chocolate, and you have yourself a date," I say.

"Happy belated Valentine's Day, Sydney," he says.

"Happy Valentine's Day."

He leans forward and kisses me again.

If you enjoyed the book, please consider leaving a review. And look for *Fourth of July Fatality*, coming soon!

You can stay up-to-date on all of Kelly's releases by subscribing to her newsletter: http://bit.ly/2pvYT07

ABOUT THE AUTHOR

Kelly Hashway fully admits to being one of the most accident-prone people on the planet, but luckily, she gets to write about female sleuths who are much more coordinated than she is. Maybe it was growing up watching *Murder, She Wrote* that instilled a love of mystery, but she spends her days writing cozy mysteries. Kelly's also a sucker for first love, which is why she writes romance under the pen name Ashelyn Drake. When she's not writing, Kelly works as an editor and also as Mom, which she believes is a job title that deserves to be capitalized.

ACKNOWLEDGMENTS

I've come to feel like a broken record at this point. My awesome team knows who they are and how much I love them, but here we go again. Patricia Bradley, thank you for jumping into another series with me. I always appreciate your feedback and your keen eye. Special thanks to Ayla Hashway for your help with the cover designs when I write too many books for one designer to handle in a year. You always bail me out.

To my VIP reader group and ARC team, thank you for sticking with me and all my characters. To my family and friends, thank you for your support and interest in my books. And finally, thank you to YOU. Yes, YOU! My readers are the absolute best, and I appreciate every single one of you.

ALSO BY USA TODAY BESTSELLING AUTHOR KELLY HASHWAY

Holidays Can Be Murder:

Valentine Victim

Traumatic Temp Agency Series:

Corpse at the Candy Shop

Piper Ashwell Psychic P.I. Series:

A Sight For Psychic Eyes

A Vision A Day Keeps the Killer Away

Read Between the Crimes

Drastic Crimes Call for Drastic Insights

You Can't Judge a Crime by its Aura

Fortune Favors the Felon

Murder is a Premonition Best Served Cold

It's Beginning to Look a Lot Like Murder

A Jailbird in the Vision is Worth Two in the Prison

Great Crimes Read Alike

I Spy With My Psychic Eye Someone Dead

A Vision in Time Saves Nine

There's No Crime Like the Prescient

Fight Fire With Foresight

Something Old, Something New, Something Foretold, Corpse So Blue

Murder Is In the Eye of the Beholder

Cup of Jo Mysteries:

Coffee and Crime

Macchiatos and Murder

Cappuccinos and Corpses

Frappes and Fatalities

Lattes and Lynching

Glaces and Graves

Espresso and Evidence

Americanos and Assault

Madison Kramer Mysteries:

Manuscripts and Murder

Sequels and Serial Killers

Fiction and Felonies

Paranormal Books:

Kiss of Death (Touch of Death Prequel)

Touch of Death (Touch of Death #1)

Stalked by Death (Touch of Death #2)

Face of Death (Touch of Death #3)

Dark Destiny

The Day I Died

Unseen Evil

Evil Unleashed

Replica

Fading Into the Shadows

Into the Fire (Into the Fire #1)

Out of the Ashes (Into the Fire #2)

Up In Flames (Into the Fire #3)

WRITING AS USA TODAY BESTSELLING ROMANCE AUTHOR ASHELYN DRAKE

Writing
as *USA Today* Bestselling Author Ashelyn Drake

The Time for Us

Second Chance Summer

It Was Always You (Love Chronicles #1)

I Belong With You (Love Chronicles #2)

Since I Found You (Love Chronicles #3)

Reignited

After Loving You (New Adult romance)

Campus Crush (New Adult romance)

Falling For You (Free prequel to *Perfect For You*)

Perfect For You (Young Adult contemporary romance)

Our Little Secret (Young Adult contemporary romance)

CONNECT WITH KELLY ONLINE

If you like connecting with authors online, you can find Kelly Hashway here:

Website: www.kellyhashway.com
TikTok: https://www.tiktok.com/@kellyhashway
Facebook: https://www.facebook.com/KellyHashwayCozy MysteryAuthor
Instagram: https://instagram.com/khashway/
Twitter: https://twitter.com/kellyhashway
Book Bub: https://www.bookbub.com/authors/kelly-hashway
YouTube: https://www.youtube.com/user/kellyhashway